TREASURE OF THE DIARY

A Mark Rollins Adventure

This is a work of fiction. While some of the names, characters, places, and incidents are products of the author's imagination and some are real, the events depicted herein are entirely fictitious and should not be considered real or factual.

ISBN: 978-1-939285-06-5 (Hardcover Edition)
ISBN: 978-1-939285-07-2 (Paperback Edition)
ISBN: 978-1-939285-08-9 (eBook Edition)

Library of Congress Control Number: 2022917470
Published by I-65 North, Inc.
Nashville, Tennessee

Cover Design by Tom Trebing

Also by M. Thomas (Tom) Collins

MARK ROLLINS ADVENTURE SERIES:

Mark Rollins' New Career & the Women's Health Club
Mark Rollins and the Rainmaker
Mark Rollins and the Puppeteer
The Claret Murders, a Mark Rollins Adventure
Diversion, a Mark Rollins Adventure
Beyond Visual Range

OTHER BOOKS:

The Language of Excellence
Exploring Asheville—Its History,
Attractions, Mysteries, Ghosts,
And Tall Tales

Acknowledgement

Thomas King Lusty was born in the United Kingdom near the village of King Stanley in the town of Stroud, Gloucestershire County on February 2, 1799, and died in the United States on August 2, 1884, at age 85. He was a ship's carpenter and, except for a short role in the Civil War building fortifications around Chattanooga, he traveled the world. Thomas Lusty, the great, great grandfather of book designer, Tom Trebing, kept a diary. It is that two-hundred-year-old diary that served as the model for the cover of this book, Treasure of the Diary.

I also want to thank the Applewood Manor for agreeing to provide rooms and delightful food and wine for the main characters of this make-believe adventure. Applewood Manor, located in the Montford Historic District, is just a short walk to the heart of downtown Asheville and is one of the city's longest continuously operating bed and breakfast style hotels.

Civil War buffs will note that I have taken liberties with certain dates and the Battle of Asheville.

Finally, I thank my wife, Martha, and my daughter, Katherine Davis, for their help with punctuation and getting all the letters in the right order. And as usual I must also recognize my wife for standing up for the reader. Her words will ring forever in my head: "You know that, but the reader doesn't—explain it."

v

TREASURE OF THE DIARY

A Mark Rollins Adventure

by

TOM COLLINS

"Wars produce many stories of fiction, some of which are told until they are believed to be true."
—Ulysses S. Grant

PROLOGUE

My name is Mark Rollins. I am a senior citizen, and according to my driver's license, I'm five feet, nine inches tall with blue eyes and brown hair. I'm a cancer survivor with a military style buzz cut—a concession to chemo. I exercise regularly in hopes that it will make me look younger than my years. I gave up fads years ago and adopted my trademark uniform: khaki trousers and black cotton polo. I've been described as a high-tech crime fighter, although I prefer to be called a problem solver.

After my investments in emerging technology industries paid off in a big way, I intended to retire. To my surprise, those retirement plans were derailed when I became the owner of the Women's Health Club located in Brentwood, a suburb of Nashville, Tennessee. The WHC is an elite, ladies-only facility for the socially prominent and wealthy. There is more to the club, however, than its glitterati clientele. It provides the cover for a clandestine problem-solving operation hidden in an annex we call "the South Forty." It houses the extensive computer and communications facilities used by my talented high-tech team that I call my Brain Trust. This clandestine side of the Women's Health Club has become extraordinarily profitable because of our unique usefulness to any number of government agencies. We operate beyond congressional oversight, and let's just say, we aren't limited by the same rules they are required to follow. Nevertheless, I can truthfully say we never seriously break the law.

My access to influential people and a penchant for adventure began in the early 1990s when the United States government asked me to help fledgling tech enterprises in Eastern Europe. Our government decided it was in our national interest to encourage emerging technologies in that part of the world. Unfortunately, governments outside the West feared technology in private hands—especially with the prevalence of the Internet. Start-up businesses were also at risk of infiltration by criminal gangs. More than once, my wife, Sarah, and I became the targets of less-than-upright people. It took more than my know-how and courageous Eastern European entrepreneurs to advance global technology in that part of the world. It also required access to powerful US government forces to crush those who would prevent or preempt its advance.

As for my designation as a problem solver, there are two kinds of problems I accept. Problems I get paid to solve—those, as noted above, come almost exclusively from segments of our government or military. The second type are those I handle pro bono for WHC members who consider me some sort of father figure or big brother. Their problems are often trivial. However, some prove dangerous—even deadly.

The diary situation that sent me and my sidekick ,Tony Caruso, to Asheville, North Carolina was one of those pro bono problems.

THE STREETS OF ASHEVILLE, NORTH CAROLINA IN THE YEAR 1865

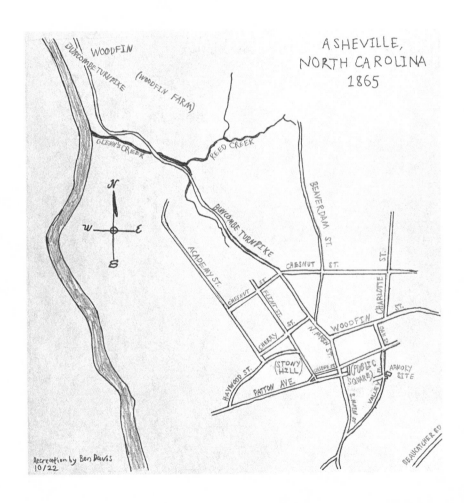

PREQUEL

It was late winter of 1865. Heavy snow had blanketed Knoxville, Tennessee, and western North Carolina. Nothing was moving on the Buncombe Turnpike in the Appalachian Mountains. After robbing the Union Army's special train, Confederate General George Andrew Welch and his remaining four men were stuck—their wagon, heavily weighted with stolen gold, made proceeding along the snow packed road impossible. There was nothing to do except wait out the weather. Luckily, there was a cabin and barn along the Turnpike where the snow had forced them to stop. The cabin belonged to Jebediah Logan who was loyal to the South and professed to hating Yankees. Logan was a hunter and trapper who lived off the land and welcomed the travelers' company with plenty of game to eat and his homemade whiskey to drink.

Not able to move, the irregular Confederate soldiers would have been an easy target for the Union troops hunting them except that they too were trapped in place by the snowfall. Unable to pursue the train robbers until the weather abated and the mountain passes cleared, Union

General Frank Blair's men cooled their heels in Knoxville's Fort Sanders.

Weeks passed before there was enough snowmelt for General Welch and his men to resume their effort to reach the Confederate stronghold of Asheville. Traveling became easier for them as their wagon moved forward traveling east and south of Knoxville. Their route was warmed by the southern sun and benefited from the natural protection of the mountains that shelter the city of Asheville from the extremes of weather.

While the train robbers were finally on the move again with their looted gold, the Union troops stationed on the northern side of the mountains were still waiting for the passes to clear.

CHAPTER 1

The Book

September 2022. Jason had that feeling again. The feeling that he was about to make a discovery. It was like an electrical shock that made him jerk and go weak in the knees just for an instant.

The book he was holding was old. There wasn't any question about that. It also was not the kind of book Belmont University would put on its library shelves. The spine, once a solid maroon was dulled by time with random colorless streaks of worn away color. The scraped and faded cover was a solid printed pattern like that of a theater curtain. Jason opened it. He turned through a few of the old pages afraid that they would crumble. One had already pulled loose from the spine. Jason loved the smell of old printed books but turning these pages fanned out a musty odor that told him this was more than old. It was ancient! The pages were handwritten in faded ink, and the cursive was so stylized that he could not make out most of the still visible words. It was indeed a journal, a diary. As he turned the pages, he again had that feeling—that sense that he was holding something of great value. He needed time to study the pages. He thought of his friend, Ella, a language major. She was a calligrapher, and he had seen her write just like this old cursive in the book. She could help him. Of course, the book might not be important. It could be nothing more than just a diary of the musings of someone who had lived a long time ago. But he felt deep down that it was the beginning of an adventure.

Jason was a sophomore majoring in Political Science and Government at Belmont University in Nashville. He worked a few hours every week in the library helping with the processing of donated books from the estates of wealthy Nashville families with personal libraries handed down through generations. People do not keep large libraries anymore. Computers changed all that. So, with no descendants interested in the family's collection of printed works stretching back generations, the elders searched for an alternative to the landfill. That alternative was usually their favorite university. Jason's job was the first stage of the intake process. He determined if a book was a duplicate of one already in the library. If it was, he segregated the book from the rest and recorded the duplicate in the "pending for sale" database.

Jason had known about Belmont's handling of donated books even before enrolling because of his part-time job at a local bookstore while still in high school. The bookstore specialized in old books usually purchased in bulk from estates or libraries, and Belmont was one of their sources. It was also that experience that got him the job in the library.

Jason was a treasure hunter at heart. It was an obsession like that of a compulsive gambler. He was always expecting a windfall discovery. He checked the coins in his pocket nightly with the expectation that one or more would be valuable. He just had a feeling that eventually someone would unknowingly give him change that included a coin of immense value. He became an avid detectorist after receiving a metal detector on his twelfth birthday. Since treasures were often found in caves, he learned spelunking. He leafed through old books and looked down their back spines for hidden money. The jobs he landed at the bookstore and at Belmont were, for him, like panning for gold. He searched every donated book for hidden treasure, and, in short order, he often would make a discovery—dried leaves, butterflies, love notes, sometimes keepsake dollar bills, money that had been hidden and then forgotten. In *The Poems of Eugene Field*, he found three one-hundred-dollar bills; but finding a single dollar bill, especially an old Silver Certificate, was enough to keep him at it—always looking for the windfall discovery that he knew, sooner or later, would come. Like all treasure hunters and gamblers, he always expected that the next search, would be the one! No matter how disappointing a day of searching books, detecting, or spelunking had been, he was convinced that the next time he would strike the mother lode!

What he was holding did not meet the definition of a published book. It was just a private diary written in longhand. Since it was not printed, there was no ISBN number or other traditional publishing information. He would be justified to trash it. After all, there was no way to catalog it. Convinced the library would not want it, under the circumstances there was nothing wrong with keeping it for himself. And there was another reason for keeping it. Long shot or not, he felt the book was the beginning of an adventure. One, he hoped, would lead him to treasure in the end.

CHAPTER 2

Three Amigos

With the faded and well-worn book in hand, Jason met Ella and his friend, Kole, in Belmont University's Student Dining Hall. The small private Christian university with 9,000 students is in the center of Nashville, Tennessee just across the street from the city's famous Music Row and a stone's throw from Vanderbilt University. The three students had instantly become friends when they met a year earlier during one of the first-year orientation events. It was now September of their sophomore year and Nashville was transitioning from a hot summer to the beginnings of fall. The leaves had not yet turned, but yellow and gold edges were beginning to appear on some of the campus trees.

Kole had eagerly embraced Jason's treasure hunting spirit becoming his spelunking partner on weekend adventures. Ella was the odd man out. She would prefer reading a book or spending her time in the library rather than climbing around inside a dark, wet cave or walking a grid on some farmland with a metal detector. Nevertheless, she was drawn to Jason's and Kole's sense of adventure. She was the research member of their three person team, and the guys did the field work. They called themselves the three amigos, and they laughed together over their treasure hunting successes and failures—mostly, of course, failures. The fact is there hadn't been any real successes—just some small finds mostly of little value, if any.

Kole and Ella had been waiting for Jason outside the dining hall when he showed up. "Hey guys, sorry I'm late. Let's go in and grab a table. I found something that you just gotta see!"

Kole said, "Don't tell me, you have discovered a treasure map!"

Ella rolling her eyes laughed, "Not another one?"

Embarrassed, Jason said, "Okay guys. I get the point. You think I am like the boy who cried wolf too many times. But this time I really think I have something special. I don't know for sure if there is really treasure involved. But I do believe it could be the beginning of an adventure. I need your help to figure it out."

Jason led them to a table away from most of the other students. "You want to get something to eat first?"

Ella replied, "Are you kidding? Eating can wait. First, I want to know what has you so excited."

"Right, who can eat when there is an adventure to be had," joked Kole.

Jason showed them the book.

Their reaction was not exactly what he expected. Kole picked it up. He slowly studied the faded and cracked front cover as Ella sitting next to him looked on. He ran his hand over the cover and examined the untitled spine on the verge of giving up its job of holding the pages together. The book clearly showed its age. It had suffered but survived. When he began leafing through the pages, they were brittle. A couple of pages were stuck together and in many spots the ink was so faded that it was illegible. The truth is all the writing was unreadable as far as Kole was concerned. Ella, watching Kole's inspection of the book, seemed much more interested even sharing a bit of Jason's excitement. She remarked, "This is very old. It looks like a diary."

"Yes, that is exactly what it is, a soldier's diary from the Civil War!" exclaimed Jason.

Kole asked, "So, it's an old, illegible diary. Other than that, what's the big deal?"

"I can't make out much of it but look at the very last entry. The longhand is hard to read. I had to study it to make it out. Just wait until you read it—you'll see why! Ella, you read it. You work with this old cursive stuff all the time. The ink in that last entry isn't as badly faded. It's still readable. Read it out loud, Ella."

Jason had the diary open to the last page with writing on it. Ella studied the cursive, reading it to herself. Then she looked at Kole and repeated the words out loud:

"I lived through it all. Stealing and hiding Atlanta Gold, killing, and being almost killed, being tortured, and almost starved to death. This part of my life is over. To remain sane, I must put it behind me. Forever over!"

CHAPTER 3

The Adventure Begins

They ate. Jason and Kole were working on cheeseburgers and fries. For Ella, it was a salad. But the talk was all about the book. Ella was the voice of reason. Was it authentic? What did Atlanta gold mean? If there was hidden gold, is it still there? Jason and Kole were already in the planning stage. There was treasure to be had! All they needed was to find out where?

Jason was the leader. "Ella, can you read this and make a transcript for us?"

She studied the book and carefully opened it turning a few pages. "I can try, but some parts are so faded, it's not going to be easy. I have a good magnifying glass that might help some." She turned back to the first page, studying what had once been beautiful handwriting. Now it was just a challenge.

Jason and Kole were watching her intently as she started to read:

Property of James Donelson Walker, corporal
CSA
If found send to my Mother Margaret Donelson
Walker, Maple Street, Nashville Tennessee.
I have four dollars hid in the seam of my---"

"I'm sorry, Jason, but I can't make out the rest of it. It's just gone—faded. The ink he used must have been home-made and has not stood the test of time. That and the heavy longhand make it illegible."

"Try the next page."

Ella turned the page as carefully as she could. A tear had already started on the first page. She studied the old, faded writing. She recognized a couple of words, but that was all. She turned another page, studying it. The boys kept their eyes on her but said nothing. "I can make out a sentence or two, but that's all," she said.

Kole said, "Read what you can."

"I can't make out the first sentence but here is some of the next part":

In February 1862 with the fall of Nashville, I got
attached to George Andrew Welch, 22nd regiment
of North Carolina that was running a hit and run
campaign against Yankee supply lines across Tennessee
and North Carolina.

She stopped reading and was scanning the rest of the page. "I can't make out the rest except for something near the end of the page." She became quiet. The guys could tell she was studying the text. She looked up, smiling at them, and said, "I think you are going to like this." The she started reading out loud:

After we hid the shipment, the General told us to scatter and blend in with the local population.

Unable to contain their excitement, Jason and Kole were leaning over the table looking intently at the page Ella was reading. All three looked up at each other with smiles on their faces. There it was, the owner of the diary, Corporal James Donelson Walker, had "hid the shipment."

Jason whispered, "You know the shipment has to be the Atlanta gold!"

No one said anything for a few minutes, then Jason said, "Guys, we must keep this just between the three of us. We are all partners in this—equal shares if anything comes of it. But I need your pledge that you will tell no one unless the three of us agree to bring that someone else into our circle of secrecy." In unison, Ella and Kole said, "Agreed!"

"Okay, we need a code word so that if we should be over-heard, we will not be giving our secret away."

Ella remarked, "Something simple and innocent."

Kole added, "Make it something about college, so it won't seem out of place."

"Good suggestion," Ella chimed in. "Why not call it a research project?"

Kole said "Sterling idea. Let's make it your project, something about the Civil War. If anyone asks Jason or me, we just say that we are helping Ella with her research project."

Ella laughed at Kole's use of air quotes around the words 'research project,' but she liked the idea and getting into the spirit, she interjected, "Let's make my project a paper dealing with Civil War prisons."

"Perfect," said Jason. "The research project is the code, and the cover is that we are helping Ella with her research on Civil War prisons."

Kole smiled, "I like it!"

Jason looking at his watch said, "I have a class in ten minutes. Everyone, think about our next steps. We can compare notes tomorrow."

CHAPTER 4

The Research Project

The three were back at the dining hall. They automatically headed towards an out of the way table. As Jason sat down, he said, "We really need to come up with someplace other than the dining hall to meet. Feeling a bit self-conscious, he added, "Sitting off by ourselves like this is just going to draw attention."

Ella volunteered, "We can use my place. I moved off campus this year, and the girl I share my apartment with is spending a semester studying at the University of Edinburgh. My place is just across the street—it's one of the first houses turned into apartments on Music Row. I've got internet and there is a small room that my roommate and I don't use. It is supposed to be a third bedroom, but it doesn't even have a closet. I think it was originally just for storage. It a has lock, actually a dead bolt. It can be our project room! We can leave our stuff out and, when we are not there, keep the room locked."

"Awesome!" Jason exclaimed. "Instead of meeting for lunch, we will just pick up something from the dining hall or Chick-fil-A and meet at the apartment. If we need more time, how about after classes? Ella, what about you?"

"I finish all my classes by four in the afternoon every day except Wednesday."

Kole volunteered, "No problem, I'm free after four o'clock any day."

"Okay," declared Jason. "We all have class demands we must stay on top of so we will take it a day at a time. We can decide about getting together after classes at our daily lunch meetings. Okay with each of you?"

Ella and Kole both indicated their agreement, and Kole spoke for all of them when he said, "Sounds like a plan!"

Kole continued, "The more I think about it, the more I believe it is important to know every word in that diary. I do not feel comfortable guessing or filling in the blanks. We think your Civil War guy hid something he called 'Atlanta gold.' But we are still assuming, and you know the old saying."

"Right," said Jason. "Assuming makes an ass out of you and me or something like that."

Ella frowned. "Yes, but how are we going to do that. I got out my magnifying glass and a strong light last night, and I still couldn't read most of what is in the book."

"I may have an answer," responded Kole. "I have been doing some research and it seems that in the Civil War era, the ink they used was homemade just as Ella had suggested. It was something called 'iron gall ink.' Believe it or not, a gall is made by an insect, a wasp. They are found on oak tree leaves. Anyway, the ink was very susceptible to fading. My research indicated that while there is no way to restore the ink on the original documents, there are methods to restore legibility through creating a facsimile. They do it by photographing the pages using UV light. The iron gall ink fluoresces as a deep black under UV light. It is time-consuming because you must keep the camera lens open for a long exposure time. Here is the thing. We either must hire someone—which means exposing our research project to a stranger. Or we get the equipment and figure out how to do this ourselves. One more thing, we would have to take the diary apart. We would need to be able to lay the pages down flat, and you cannot do that without destroying the book."

Jason said, "I hadn't thought about that. I do know a little about UV photography. It takes specialized cameras and working with ultraviolet light is tricky and can be danger-ous if you don't know what you are doing. The library has a conservation lab, and it includes an ultraviolet photography setup used to digitize historic documents. Since I am on the library staff, I can probably get permission to use it in off hours. We just need our own SIM card to store the images."

Ella asked, "Won't they want to know what you're doing?"

"No worries, I'll just use our cover story." Talking like a robot, he repeated their agreed cover story. "I—am—help-ing—a—friend—with—her—research—on—Civil—War—prisons." Once he stopped laughing at his own joke, Jason continued, "And I tell them that I'm photographing some old letters and other documents from the period."

Ella shook her head as she sarcastically said, "Ha, ha, you're so funny."

Kole's mind had been running ahead thinking about next steps. "Seriously, any idea how long this will take, Jason?"

"I won't know until I have tried it. I doubt I can use the lab for more than an hour at a time without raising ques-tions. Just to be on the conservative side, maybe I can get one or two pages a night—maybe more. If I had to guess—I would say it will take about two weeks to photograph all the pages. However, Ella will be transcribing pages as we go. So, we should have the full readable transcript of the diary within two weeks."

Ella asked, "Do you want me to take the book apart?"

"How would you do it?" asked Jason.

"I don't know. Maybe with a razor blade?"

"No, after thinking about it, I would rather you, as our research arm, see what you can find out about Atlanta gold. What was our Confederate corporal referring to? What was the shipment? What was it worth? Kole, I would like you to take the book apart. Use an X-ACTO knife to remove the pages with writing on them without destroying the book itself. Try to leave a little of the left margin attached to the book's spine so we can tape it back together. Also, be sure to number the pages you remove, or we will never get the thing back together with the pages in the right order. There are a lot of blank pages still left in the book, and I want to preserve as much of the old diary's structure as possible."

CHAPTER 5

Jason McConnell

Jason is a fairly nice looking young man with blue eyes and dark hair worn in a preppy or formal style parted on the side. He is a lanky six feet tall and trim. You would not call him muscular, but he is strikingly fit. Unless it's too cold or a special occasion, he usually wears traditional blue jeans, T-shirt, and New Balance or plain toe laced boots.

His father, Gregory Hyatt McConnell, at five feet eight inches and two hundred thirty four pounds is fifty-two years old. Greg, as he prefers to be called, is a fundamentalist Christian. But he is also the top earning patent lawyer in the country focused on high-stakes cases involving complicated technology and mission-critical cases in the entertainment industry. He is also a renowned poker champion. In short, he is not a man you want on the opposing side if you are involved in litigation. He expected his only child, Jason Stewart McConnell, to follow in his footsteps as a lawyer.

Unfortunately, that was not Jason's plan. Instead, he leaned toward his father's poker playing side. Before enrolling at Belmont University, he got his spending money

17

playing poker with guys in the neighborhood—the wealthy Brentwood, Tennessee area called the Governor's Club. When he wasn't in school or playing poker, he was hunting for treasure at the bookstore where he was working part-time. He had discovered that old books sometimes contained hidden money or other objects. He also found time to go treasure hunting in area caves and using his metal detector on some farm or antebellum estate.

Jason's mother is the former Jennifer Welham. At forty-two, she is ten years younger than her husband and prior to marriage, she was Greg's legal secretary. The Welhams are old Nashville money and live in the Belle Meade home that Jennifer's grandfather built as the family compound. She attended a private girls' high school then Vanderbilt University and went to work at Greg's law firm right after graduating with a bachelor's degree in liberal arts. She still wears the same size dress she wore when she graduated, and she keeps her attractive, slender figure by working out daily at the Women's Health Club in Brentwood.

The college issue was driving a wedge between father and son. Jennifer tried to be the peacemaker. Jason's father was convinced that his son would come around to his way of thinking as he got a little older and money became more important. Jason didn't really know, yet, how he was going to afford to pursue his interest as a treasure hunter. But like any gambler, treasure hunter, or dreamer, he was convinced it would work out. He just had to keep searching for that pot of gold at the end of the rainbow. Sooner or later, he would find it!

Jen, as she prefers to be called even by her son, negotiated a truce. Jason agreed to enroll in Belmont in Prelaw or Political Science for at least two years. At the end of those two years, Jason would have the option of continuing to work toward a law degree or not. If he decided to stick with it, Greg would continue to pay for college and law school. On the other hand, if Jason decided to do his own thing, he would do so with the understanding that he would have to support himself.

Everyone seemed happy with the compromise. At least for now.

CHAPTER 6

The Project Room

By day three, Kole had transformed Ella's spare room into a well-equipped workroom. A large white board was now on the wall. He had added two sixty-inch worktables, the folding type along with comfortable plastic chairs. But the best was his addition of two new Dell laptop computers and a HP combination laser printer and scanner. As for where it all came from, Kole wasn't saying, and the others weren't asking. Jason and Ella had become accustomed to Kole's ability to suddenly acquire supplies and equipment just when it was needed.

They assumed he had a trust fund or some source of income that he did not like to talk about. There was a good reason to believe that. Kole was an enigma. He spoke with a slight European accent. His English was a bit more British than American, but there was a toughness about the way he spoke. It was the kind of thing that made you think he probably carried a weapon in his pocket. When it came to his clothes, even though he wore the same things as everybody else—T-shirts, pants, and canvas shoes—he looked different, better. His tees came from Lululemon and instead of jeans, he wore ABC Pants, and his Converse shoes were always the most stylish or hip. He had thick, brushed back hair and stood five feet eleven inches tall. He had a formal air about him in that his posture, walking or seated, was just better than everyone else's, even princely or more like a military officer.

In addition to remaking their workroom, Kole had also completed his assigned task, cutting out the pages from the book that had writing on them. He had carefully numbered each page with a blue flair felt tipped pen and placed each sheet in its own buffered, acid and lignin free file folder. Then he placed them in a Gaylord Archival Clamshell Preservation Box. Going above and beyond what was expected of him was his standard operating procedure. And since he had gotten the box to Jason yesterday in plenty of time to use the library lab equipment, he was expecting him to arrive this morning with one or two UV photos.

Ella was working on her usual lunch dish, another salad, and in between bites was telling Kole about her research when Jason arrived with the first UV photograph. It was Page Number One.

As Jason sat down, he exclaimed, "Wow! Kole! You have really put things together. It is quite a conversion and I know we have you to thank for all of this stuff."

"Not bad work, if I say so myself," smiled Kole. "I hereby christen it as Ella's Project Room."

"So be it," replied Jason. Ella smiled approvingly.

Kole explained, "The white board is magnetic. I thought we could use it to post the photographs. There are magnets in the basket at the bottom, on the right."

Jason grabbed one of the small magnets and began posting the photograph. "Getting permission took a couple of days but last night I finally was able to produce our first UV page." The posted document was remarkably clear. Text that had been faded and almost completely unreadable, now appeared as dark clear handwriting.

Ella began studying the UV image. "As I retype these, I will put them in Microsoft's Cloud with a password. That way we can all have access. Any ideas for the password?" The three just looked at each other. After their long pause, Ella said, "How about 09021864?"

Kole asked, "What's that?"

"It is the date of the fall of Atlanta, September 2, 1864."

"That works for me," said Jason.

Kole agreed, "Consider it a done deal—make it so, girl!"

Pleased, Ella smiled as she said, "Okay everybody, listen up. I am going to read Page One":

Property of James Donelson Walker, corporal CSA
If found send to my Mother Margaret
Donelson Walker, Maple Street,
Nashville Tennessee.

I have four dollars hid in the seam of my Richmond and used a dollar of it to buy ink, pen, and this journal and then another twenty-five cents for a used Haversack to hold them. All I purchased from a Sutler who had managed to get his wagon to the Island. I determined to keep this Journal for my mother who I may never again see. If I should die in this God forsaken

*place and have no marker for my grave at least
she may have this journal to remember me by.*

After reading the fancy cursive script, Ella waited for a reaction.

It was Jason who spoke. "What the devil is a Richmond or a Sutler for that matter. And how about a Haversack?"

Kole was typing on one of the Dell computers. "According to Wikipedia a sutler is a civilian merchant who sells provisions to an army in the field, in camp, or in quarters. Sutlers sold wares from the back of a wagon. And, a Haversack, 'have r sack,' is what it sounds like. It is a cloth sack that was made water resistant. The soldiers carried their food in it."

Ella said, "I know the answer to the Richmond question. It was a jacket style worn by Confederate soldiers—like the Eisenhower jackets in WWII."

Jason said, "Well, this first page does not tell us much. Maybe the next one will be more interesting. Ella, any luck with your research regarding Atlanta gold?"

"Not yet, I subscribed to the *New York Times* database and have started reading their 1864 editions dealing with the Battle of Atlanta in July 1864. I hope I will have something by tomorrow."

A little disappointed, Jason rose as he said, "Okay, let's call it a day. I will see if I can get into the conservation lab tonight and photograph a couple more pages. Now that I have done one, it should go a lot faster."

CHAPTER 7

Atlanta Gold

Jason used the key Ella had given him and was about to post the new pages on the white board when Kole arrived, as promised, with three fried chicken salads from Chick-Fil-A. Ella was the last to arrive carrying printouts, copies from 1864 editions of *The New York Times*.

Ella retrieved three bottles of water from the refrigerator and the guys sat down and started on their salads. Eager to report on her research of Atlanta gold, Ella pushed hers aside for later. "I found two news articles that are related. I am still looking for more, however." She handed them copies of her printouts. "The first is a copy of a short article reporting on something that originally appeared in the *Atlanta Constitution*. Let me read it":

> Atlanta, Georgia. September 29, 1864—The *Constitution* has learned that a special military train was set upon by a gang of robbers between Chattanooga and Monteagle, Tennessee. The source who asked to remain anonymous is a

member of the military unit that was guarding a shipment of gold bullion being transferred from the Bank of Atlanta to the Union Bank in Memphis.

She continued without slowing, "It doesn't specifically say Atlanta gold, but it is the right time period." Becoming more excited, she stood pacing. "The second article is the clincher! It refers to the same train robbery. Just listen to this":

Atlanta, October 2, 1864—A shipment of 20,000 troy ounces of confiscated Confederate gold being taken by a special military train from Atlanta to Memphis is missing. The gold was stolen by train robbers who after a bloody gun fight were able to uncouple the last car from the moving train. It was the mail car and contained the gold shipment. Mr. Will Brownly, a local farmer, is said to have come upon the mail car lying on its side, after it had apparently jumped the track. Five well-armed men commandeered the farmer's wagon and four pulling horses. Mr. Brownly observed five crates as they were transferred with great effort from the mail car to his wagon. The farmer, who was unharmed in the incident, said the men wore remnants of Confederate uniforms leading him to believe that they were deserters. Major General Frank Blair, whose men under his command guarded the shipment, is said to have vowed to hunt down the perpetrators and recover the missing gold. The Union guards on the train suffered heavy losses from the surprise attack but are said to have killed or captured at least a dozen of the train robbers.

Kole had shoved his half eaten salad aside and was keying on the computer. "A troy ounce of gold is worth almost eighteen hundred dollars. That means we are talking about thirty-six million dollars of hidden gold."

"Right," said Ella. "And if you are wondering, that is more than half a ton of gold. The gold bars used by banks at that time each weighed twenty-five pounds. So, the Atlanta gold shipment must be fifty bars. If there were five crates, each with ten bars, then each crate weighed two hundred fifty pounds. All together that's one thousand two hundred fifty pounds of gold." Smiling, she quipped, "Now that's a lot of bullion!"

Jason's legs were tingling again. It was that electrical shock he experienced just before a discovery. At first neither Kole nor Jason said anything. They needed time to fully comprehend the significance of Ella's words—what they meant for the three of them. But they were both smiling.

CHAPTER 8

Ship Island

Jason broke the silence. "I guess you can't call me the boy who cried wolf anymore, can you?" Rising from his chair and walking to the white board smiling, he continued, "This time there really is a treasure—a thirty-six million dollar one!" He began posting the new UV photographs. "I was able to move much faster now that I have gotten the hang of the UV process."

Ella moved to the board. After a moment she began reading one page to the next without pausing, but at times she hesitated as she untangled the loops and curves of the heavy cursive writing.

Diary Page 2
I was twenty-two when I was mustered into the Confederate Army in Nashville, assigned to the 10th Regiment, Tennessee Infantry Company F under Captain Randall W. McGavock as a corporal considering my prior four years duty in the Tennessee Militia.

29

In February 1862 with the fall of Nashville, I got attached to George Andrew Welch, 22nd regiment of North Carolina that was running a hit and run campaign against Yankee supply lines across Tennessee and North Carolina. There wasn't much left of the 22nd and at some point, after the Union pretty much occupied all of Tennessee, I think we accidently stopped being an actual part of the army of the Confederate States of America. We had good Union horses and mules we had stolen, Union boots, tack gear and provisions. Some of us had replaced our worn out pants with Union pants but we always wore our CSA blouses and Richmond jackets no matter how tattered they had become.

Just before I was captured, there was only five of us left and we were on the run from Yankees after we intercepted one of their shipments that they had looted from Atlanta. After we hid the shipment, the General told us to scatter and blend in with the local population because we were cut off and there was no way we were going to outrun the Union men. I don't know what happened to my General or the rest of the men. I was captured by the Yankees in the winter of '64 while I was still near Asheville, North Carolina, and after some months of moving from confinement camps and jails, I was sent here to Ship Island off the coast of Mississippi. I think one of the locals ratted me out and sent me to hell. No, hell is surely better than this vile place.

Diary Page 3

When the transport bringing me here approached the island, its pure white sand sparkled like a jewel. It was the whitest sand I had ever seen, and it removed my fear of being imprisoned. I was going to a beautiful beach. It all came to an awful end as we docked, and my feet touched the sandy ground. I could smell the prison camp. It was the smell of rot as foul as any pig farm mingled with that of dead bodies like that on the battlefield. It is a smell you never forget. There had been about forty of us on the sailboat. We were taken inland and marched through the gate of this place—the first thing I saw was a ditch dug in the sand with a dozen dead souls stretched out waiting to be covered over. There were no coffins not even boards covering the men.

Diary Page 4

Most of the guards were black. When they brought us into the parade ground and closed the gate behind us, my eyes fell on so many men and so much misery. Poor souls—yellowed faces and bug eyed—many were walking dead. The lack of humanity laid waste to the beauty of the snow white sand. My mind couldn't grasp it. How can such beauty under foot be so dreadfully spoiled by the filth, sickness, and death above it? The guards made no record of us. There was no assignment to quarters. There were no quarters—no shelter of any kind. Men lived on the sand, and I quickly learned that the white sand was no friend. By the time the sun rose halfway to noon in the mornings, it became as hot as a stove top. Most men had no blankets, no cover to get away from the burning sun and sand. Yet it turned cold when the sun left us. Don't ever think it don't get cold in the South. This may be part of Mississippi, but it is an island—wind and wet fog from the sea makes for a miserable night. Men huddled together at night for warmth from the wet, cold air off the waters. They had a system of rotation to the edges of their huddles.

Diary Page 5

Many men are barefoot and if they found rags, they used them to wrap their bare feet or they would blister their feet on the fiery hot sand. You sleep with your boots on if you have them. If you took off your boots, someone would quickly steal them. Men were willing to fight and die over a pair of boots. We suffer greatly from the sand. It is so fine that it floats in the air like snowflakes and gets in your eyes, hair, nose, ears, and your food and drink. Our pants, blouses, and feet are never free from the irritating sand.

Diary Page 6

I cannot write every day. I am afraid the guards will take my journal away, so I wait until I'm sure I am out of a guard's view. Sometimes

that is a week or more. I think this is my thir-
teenth week. I may have lost count. When I am
not writing, I bury the journal, pen and ink in
the sand using my Haversack. While we can
write letters, they can be no more than a single
page and they must be read and approved by the
officer in charge. The men say, they think most
letters never go beyond the prison gate. I keep
my journal and things hidden and out of the
weather because if the guards didn't take them
the rain and wind surely would. There was a
miracle today—the guards brought tents and
piled them in the parade ground. There were a
lot. Each big enough for eight to ten men. All
damaged in some way. Some suffered from gun
and cannon shot, others with rot and tears, but
each was a Godsend. There were enough for all,
but there were still many fights.

Diary Page 7

Today, another prisoner was killed for
touching the dead line. That's a strand of wire
about six feet from the stockade wall. The wire
is nailed on boards about fifty feet apart and
circles the entire stockade. It is to keep anyone
from getting close to the wall in an escape
attempt. If a man steps over the line or just
touches it, the guards have orders to shoot to
kill. Our guards seem eager to do so. Today a
man who was sick and near delirious staggered
too close to the dead line and stumbled into it.
He was shot in the head. Later I realized that

might have been his good luck. He died a fast painless death versus what surely would have been a miserable one from whatever disease he was suffering from. People do not get well here. They get sick and they die. We have men with cholera, malaria, and TB. God help me!

This tale of misery left all three feeling drained. It took a few silent moments before anyone spoke.

Finally, Kole did. "What about the gold? None of this tells us enough, just that he hid it. We already know that. Maybe we should have started from the end of the journal and worked to the beginning."

Ella said, "Patience, Kole. We have just begun. There is a lot that we haven't read yet."

Jason agreed, "Ella is right, Kole. Remember you were the one who said we should have the complete text before doing anything. If we only deciphered pieces, we might miss the most important clue for finding the Atlanta gold."

"Yeah, you guys are right. Let's stick to the plan."

CHAPTER 9

Dreaming of Gold

Fall break was approaching. Jason and Kole had been hoping that they could hunt for the treasure during the break, but that meant they had to learn where to look first. And they still had not found that answer yet. The frustration was building as they continued their daily meetings in Ella's project room.

Today, Ella raised a question, "If we did find it, would it be ours? Or could the Government or some bank in Atlanta claim the gold is theirs? I hate to bring it up. It's just that I started worrying about that, and we need to find out."

Kole suggested, "There must be rules about buried treasure. How about the law library?"

"Right," added Jason. "Ella, why don't you take that on. See if you can find out the rules regarding discovery of hidden gold, or treasure, which may have been stolen more than 150 years ago?"

"Okay," she said as she began studying the new pages. "Kole, you get your wish today. Our prisoner finally mentions the gold again!"

Diary Page 8

It is now the end of February or the first of March by my calculations. My journal has been hidden away for some time. We had gotten all new black guards. The old guards got where they didn't care much if we broke some of the rules. The new guards seem intent to hold us to rules—some I think they make up to torment us. Also new men were added to my tent. Cholera had freed up some cots and two of them just made space on the sand floor for their blankets. I was afraid that one of the new prisoners might turn me in for extra food, a blanket, or a hat. And I didn't know what the replacement guards might do to me.

Diary Page 9

I am writing again. I found that none of the new black replacements, all former slaves, could read or write. And frankly, they did not fare much better than we prisoners. Their uniforms were still intact where ours were, at best, badly worn. They also had first opportunity to any provisions that arrived by ship. But they also got sick from the poor food and water, and they died too. I heard that one of the guards killed himself last night. Shot himself through the mouth. There is no better care taken for their burial. But at least they have markers for their graves, while we have none. After much consideration, I decided to recover the journal and get back to writing down what might be the end of my life. If I do not die of disease, I surely will of starvation before long.

Diary Page 10
We have suffered from many rainstorms off the sea. From rain and heavy fog, we are seldom dry in the mornings. But last night was the worst. It was a terrible storm! Many of the tents were blown away or damaged. Lightning struck a tent only four tents from ours and three men were killed and another seven were stunned or hurt in some way. The next day, every creeping thing that flies, or crawls emerged to torture us all. They got in your hair and mouth and found ways into your clothes. They bit and stung and there was no escape.

Diary Page 11
We get food only once a day now. The guards bring it in using a two-wheel wagon and dumped it on the sand. Every man is on his own. If you are late to the pile or too ill to get there, you went without. Most of the time it was cornbread made mostly from corncobs. Sometimes there was foul smelling half-cooked pork or bacon not fit for human consumption, but if you got some you consumed it anyway. The bottom of the pile was covered in sand. You wiped the food the best you could, but you ate it sand and all. Whatever you got—you ate right then. There was no saving for later. Water was brackish and bad. The smelly stuff had to be

brought by ship and was taken from streams on the mainland of Mississippi. Streams that had been fouled by cattle and worse. Every day ten to twelve men died and get laid in the burial ditches with no markers or record of their death.

Diary Page 12
One of the men found a way to get fresh water today. We found a barrel and buried it down about two feet and it filled with pure sweet water. The guards learned what we had done and came and took the barrel for themselves.

Diary Page 13
I dreamed of the gold last night. It cost the lives of many friends. Now the South is lost, too. And all for what—gold we sent back to Mother Earth.

CHAPTER 10

Finders Keepers

Ella handed two printouts from the computer to the guys.
"I found another newspaper article about the gold shipment,
and I researched North Carolina laws dealing with treasure
hunting. Let me read the article first":

Knoxville, Tennessee—*The Brownlow's Knoxville
Whig*; November 15, 1865.

Union troops in pursuit of the Confederate
deserters who made off with a shipment of gold
in a September train robbery are on the move
again. The Union troops under the command
of General Frank Blair were delayed some six
weeks due to heavy snow and ice blocking
roads in the Appalachian Mountains of western North Carolina. The fugitives are believed
to be in route to the Confederate held city of
Asheville, North Carolina.

"But do the bloody Union troops catch up with the Confederates?" asked Kole.

Jason observed, "The article is another confirmation that the gold is real and that their destination is the area around Asheville. But Kole is right. We do need to know more about the Union troops pursuing them. So, we need to keep looking."

"I agree," Ella said. "I installed an APT that crawls around in the cloud looking for key words I have given it. So, the search goes on around-the-clock. Now for the rules dealing with treasure hunting. While I am not a lawyer, I think if we find it, we get to keep it—less income taxes, of course."

"Of course," exclaimed Jason. "Death and taxes are the only two certainties in this world!"

"Back to what the research yielded—this is what I found. Generally, the law favors 'finders, keepers' with some exceptions. First, what we find or dig up, must qualify as treasure. For example, if you find someone's wallet you cannot keep it. If someone can claim and prove ownership, then ownership rules. In our case, the gold was the property of the Confederate States which no longer exist and, therefore, cannot claim ownership. Next, if discovered items are considered antiquities, one hundred years old or older, and are found on federal or state land, then it is subject to North Carolina's Antiquities Act. From what we have found so far, the buried gold is not going to be on state or federal land. And even if it was, gold bars from the eighteen hundreds can hardly be considered antiquities, can it?"

"Good work," remarked Jason. "I can, however, see one possibility that might muddy the waters. The U.S. government might assert that the gold had been confiscated for war reparations prior to shipment. So, keep your eye to the ground, so to speak. See if there are any precedents. You may not be a lawyer yet, but in my book, I think you would make a great one."

"Actually, I have been thinking about it. I really like being in the law library."

Kole chimed in, "You should go for it." Then his impatience showing, he continued, "How about the new UV photographs. Have you read them yet? Anything there to help us?"

Ella, moved to the white board with the posted pages. "Let me read them out loud":

Diary Page 14
Two weeks have gone by without any food from the guards. I managed to snare a black skimmer with a bad wing. There was very little meat to be had after plucking it and no way to cook it. I chewed it and thought it was the best food I ever had. The truth be told a rock, if there was one on this damn island, would have tasted grand as well. The feathers, I saved hoping to make something useful from it.

Diary Page 15
The officer in charge shot five men today. One has since died. They were congregating, he said.

Diary Page 16
Today, the guards dumped a load of wood and lumber in the middle of the camp, and we scrambled to get a share. It was a strange thing seeing walking skeletons fighting over pieces

of wood. The boats that brought men to the island also brought rats. The rats were around the garbage piles that were more human waste than food—we had eaten all the food there was. Rats also hung around the death ditches. All the men went hunting for those rats. They were using pieces of wood as their weapons. The rats were so accustomed to being around us prisoners that they did not even run. Then some of the men managed to get a fire going. Let me tell you, that night the entire camp had roasted rat. If you been starved for a long time, you will think you have gone to heaven. That rat feast was like thanksgiving. And it was the first time I had seen happy men. They even got to singing until the guards got tired of it and just started shooting. Four men were killed that night, but they died happy.

Jason reported, "That is all I could photograph last night. The conservation people worked late. So, I did not get in the lab until very late. I am getting better at reading the corporal's cursive. I looked ahead in the diary while waiting for the lab and from what little I could make out; the next few pages are going to tell us a lot."

"Good," shouted Kole. "I say, let's get this thing on the road. I'm ready to go treasure hunting!"

CHAPTER 11

Directions to the Gold

Ella and Jason were already in the project room when Kole arrived. Jason, who was still in the process of posting pages photographed the previous night, grumbled. "Damn it, Kole why don't you have an iPhone?"

Kole shook his head and said, "I do just fine without the minute to minute interruptions of mobile phone calls and texts."

"Well, it was your loss! Last night's photos are what we have been looking for—exciting stuff. I really wanted to share the news, but you have chosen not to have a damn phone!"

Ella was up and staring at the new pages. "This is what you call a smoking gun."

Kole almost screamed, "Guys, you are killing me! Get on with it. Please read it."

"Okay, okay," responded Ella. "Here we go":

Diary Page 17
*I just don't see how I can make it much
longer. So weak, writing is hard to do. I fear the*

end is near and with the growing belief that our Dixieland is losing to the Union—it is best I that write about the shipment in hopes this book of mine will make it to my mother and through her to my sister, Gemma, whose strength of character has been the backbone of our family. If I should die in this Godforsaken place, I do so with the knowledge that Gemma shall care for my mother.

I was right proud to be part of General Welch's troop. I was told he graduated West Point, second in the class of 1850. Resigned his commission in '61 to accept command of the 22nd Regiment, North Carolina Infantry as Brigadier General in the Confederate Army. We were loyal Southern boys. But as I look back on it, we had become guerillas living off the land with what we could steal or what people would give us. There were wanted posters for us. We were considered deserters by the South and outlaws by the North. And the General's poster was for dead or alive.

Somehow General Welch received word, from certain Confederate assets, that some of the Confederate wealth held in Atlanta banks was being shipped by rail through Union controlled Nashville to Memphis where it was to be deposited to accounts of the United States Treasury. By that time, our troop was down to about twenty men. But they were seasoned fighters and we set off to capture the shipment for the South. Our plan was to attack the train west of Chattanooga as it started up the steep climb to Monteagle, Tennessee. The tracks there follow along the Mountain Goat trail. It's called that for good reason. At that point, the train speeds would be reduced to a crawl due to the sharp incline up Monteagle Mountain.

Diary Page 18

I was telling about our attack on the train. Union soldiers heavily guarded its cargo. About fourteen men of our troop were killed or wounded in the gun fight, but the General and a handful of us managed to fight our way into the last car on the train, the mail car, where the shipment was being held. And one of our men, it was Bobby Pierce, was able to uncouple the mail car from the rest of the train. That car went flying back down the mountain track. It jumped the rails as it was getting near the bottom crashing us all. We lost another man in the crash. After the fight and the wreck of the mail car there wasn't much left of us. The General and four of us stole a wagon from a farmer. We loaded the cargo on the wagon and headed to Confederate held western North Carolina expecting the Yankees to be hot on our tails.

Diary Page 19

About our trek to North Carolina, we might surely have benefitted from another plan cause getting to Asheville was easier said than done. It took us months. We could easily have not made

45

it at all and froze to death, not to be found until the spring snowmelt. But we were a determined lot and we pushed on. We knew Asheville was a major center for the CSA and would be well armed and fortified. We thought we could deliver our prize and get pardoned and be safe from the Union Soldiers that was chasing us. You might say we looked at the gold as the price we were paying to get our lives back. At one point, the snows had us stopped altogether for a good six weeks. We figured the Union troops chasing us could not do any better. The snow would have them stopped too.

Diary Page 20

One of the black guards fired shots into our tent last night and killed a young boy from Memphis. William Tyler was his name. There was no reason!

Diary Page 21

Getting back to our mission, we finally got to Asheville, cold and road tired, only to find that the CSA military had pulled out. What we did not know was that the Union attacked Asheville in August. And after a brief fight, they pulled out bypassing Asheville for Charlotte and then Raleigh, the capital. Asheville's Confederate force withdrew to counterattack the Yankees from their rear. The canons on the hill that had been Patton Battery were gone. The armory where we had been making rifles was aban-

doned. There were plenty of battlements dug to protect the city especially around Glenn's Creek and where Camp Patton had been.

They had even dug tunnels as part of the city's defenses and to store gun powder and supplies. Big ones had been dug from the armory to Patton Battery and to where Camp Patton had been. There was still black powder in one of the tunnels. There was one tunnel that was being dug from College Street running parallel to the Turnpike going northwest toward the battlements around Glenn's Creek, but it was not finished. The lift and pully system were still in place. The General had us lower the cargo down into that tunnel. We used the excavation wagons to haul the Atlanta shipment to the end of the unfinished tunnel. I stepped it off and it was 352 paces. We knew we were boxed in and were likely to be killed or captured. So, we decided that if we could not get the gold to the Confederacy, we at least did not want the North to get their hands on that treasure after so many of us had died for it. So, the General blew up the tunnel burying the Atlanta bank shipment where no one was going to find it. After blowing up the tunnel, the General told us to scatter. Every man on his own.

Kole let out a big whistle. "There it is man! The bloke might as well have given us a map. We got the directions. It is time to do a little digging."

47

Jason said, "Not so fast, Kole. There are just a few more pages and then we will be finished with the diary. Let's stick to the plan. We don't want to overlook something in his journal that might bite us in the rear because we missed it."

Ella added, "Yes, and we have been so busy hoping to find these directions that we have not given any thought to the next steps. I mean now that we know where to look, what is our plan?"

"Ella is right. So, Kole, why don't you take the planning task—when, where, how, et cetera. When do we go on our treasure hunt? What do we need—what tools? How do we travel? Where do we stay? What to tell people?"

"Okay, but I'll need input from you and Ella."

"Get a darn phone!" Jason did not really expect him to do it.

CHAPTER 12

Forever Over

On Saturday, the weather had changed—the first really cold day of the fall season. Since there were no classes scheduled, they met early. There was coffee and Ella had a purchased a mixture of original and chocolate glazed Krispy Kreme doughnuts for their session. Kole skipped the coffee and poured himself a glass of milk from Ella's refrigerator.

Jason posted the final pages from the diary of James Donelson Walker, Corporal CSA, and Ella began reading:

Diary Page 22
It is late April 1865, and we were being marched to ships. I was put on a steamship and told we were going to Vicksburg to be exchanged for Union prisoners. Grown men were crying from happiness. But we were leaving a lot of men behind buried in ditches made in the sand and others who were too sick or too weak

49

to walk to the ships. I doubt they ever left the island in this life.

Diary Page 23

In Vicksburg, we got word that Robert E. Lee surrendered his troops to Union General Ulysses S. Grant at Appomattox Court House in Virginia on the ninth of April '65. The War was over. I was given a pardon document, a rifle, and a few provisions and was free to return home to my beloved Nashville. Or what was left of it. I decided to make no more entries in this journal.

I lived through it all. Stealing and hiding Atlanta gold. Killing men and being almost killed by other men. Being tortured and almost starved to death. This part of my life is over! To remain sane, I must put that life and the gold behind me. Forever over!

The three sat silent for few minutes then Jason spoke. "Well, that answers an important question."

Ella asked, "What's that?"

It was Kole who answered her. "That he didn't go back to Asheville and dig up the gold."

"That's right!" Jason slapped the tabletop. "For Corporal Walker it was 'Forever Over.' Now it's up to us to dig up that gold! So, Kole what have you come up with. Lay it on us. What is the plan?"

CHAPTER 13

Ella Blakeford

Ella Grace Blakeford grew up in the Evergreen Historic District of Memphis, Tennessee. The home on Forrest Avenue had expanded over the years with additions. Her parents regularly remodeled the kitchen, bathrooms, and the rest of the house to keep them up to date and in vogue with current styles. The last addition was a swimming pool and guest house all behind a new seven foot brick wall. They entertained in a beautiful oak paneled room with a full bar and a circular stair leading down to a well-stocked wine cellar. And they entertained often. Ella's father, Dr. Howard Blakeford, was a philosophy professor and her mother, Dr. Carol Blakeford, whose inherited fortune came from her father's early investments in Holiday Inn, was head of the English department. Both were tenured at Memphis State University. The University campus was a short four and a half miles from their home.

Ella Blakeford was an only child conceived early in the Blakeford marriage. Both parents quickly decided that raising children was a distraction from their academic interests and vowed to have no more. The distraction of raising the child they already had, Ella, was solved with live-in au pairs until Ella's last two years of high school when her parents decided she could get by on her own.

Ella attended Harding Academy, a coeducational Christian day school, from her kindergarten days to her graduation from high school. The Academy is close to the University and is considered one of the city's best private schools.

Ella grew up in a liberal and affluent bubble. Sheltered, you might say, from the masses. She made straight A's. That was expected of her. She did little in the way of sports and spent her time in academic pursuits because that what Blakefords did, and high grades and intellectual accomplishments were what was expected of her. As she got older, and especially by the time she was in her last two years at the Academy, she began to envy her classmates who were more adventurous. She realized how much she was missing by focusing so exclusively on intellectual pursuits. In her senior year, she found a boyfriend, Gene Ellsworth, and finally began joining classmates at sports events and parties.

While her parents expected her to go to Memphis State, she was determined not to. She wanted to get away from the "expectations." Gene was enrolling in Nashville's Belmont University, majoring in Music Business. So that is what Ella did. She enrolled at Belmont. Her parents agreed because they believed in letting Ella make her own decisions no matter how much her decisions disappointed them. And they let her know they had expected more loyalty to their Memphis State University.

Early on, Gene discovered beer, Nashville's lower Broadway music district, and girls who also liked Broadway and getting wasted. He lost interest in Ella and his drinking and trips to the Broadway District became more important that attending classes. He was suspended by the University for cause, including non-attendance, after being there for only two months. By the time Gene packed up and returned to Memphis, Ella had met and befriended Jason and Kole. She no longer cared about her former boyfriend, and she enjoyed the freedom from her parents' expectations.

CHAPTER 14

The Plan

Their excitement still running high, the three adventurers were meeting again on a Saturday. It was early morning. Ella got out her Pop-Tart assortment. Jason now knew how to use Ella's Nespresso machine and made coffee. Kole brought his beverage from Starbucks. Truth is no one was very hungry. Kole sipped his Royal English Breakfast Tea, took a bite of a Frosted Chocolate Fudge Pop-Tart, and stood up assuming a professorial stance.

"We have fall break in one week from today. It's time to go to Asheville. Jason, can we use your Acura MDX? With three of us going and all of our equipment, we need a four by four—of course, I know you call them SUVs."

"Sure! It's not new. Mine is a 2010 with a hundred and twenty thousand miles on it, but the tires are good, and I just had it serviced."

"Excellent. The next question is can everyone go? Ella, any problem taking your fall break with two guys."

"No, my parents are so liberal they voted for Biden. Two guys will not bother them. They would think that is bold of me. But they would be even happier if I were going with a couple of trans or non-binaries."

Jason could not help saying, "I guess they are happy about Biden cancelling student debt. What a dope! My dad is mad as hell about it. What about your folks, Kole?"

"Don't care one way or the other but back to our plan. What about a base of operation? Where shall we stay?"

Jason was eager to answer. "I have an idea. At least it will work for a few days. After that we can decide our other options, including camping. My parents went to a charity event and bid on a stay at a bed and breakfast that happens to be in Asheville, and they won. I knew they were planning a trip to Provence in France. So, I asked them if we could use the B&B for fall break. They said okay. It's called the Applewood Manor, and it's supposed to be within walking distance of the downtown area where we believe the gold is. The only problem is we would have to double up—all stay in the same room."

"Okay by me, what about you, Ella?" asked Kole.

Giggling, she said, "Sure, but I get the bed. You guys can have the couch or the floor. And I get first dibs on the bathroom!"

"That is nothing new for us guys," joked Kole. "Girls always get first choice, and we are experts at waiting and waiting and waiting. However, back to the plan. Applewood Manor it is! Everyone has agreed to go on this adventure, and transportation and the base of operation are settled. Next, we need to update our cover story. The prison thing won't work for our Asheville trip. I suggest we switch to helping Ella investigate Asheville's military role in the Civil War. Here, let me rephrase it. Ella Blakeford's thesis is on the military role of Asheville in the Civil War, and we guys—detectorists—volunteered to help her look for Civil War artifacts that support her thesis."

Sighing, Ella asked, "Why is it always me?"

Continuing Kole said, "It's easier for people to believe. Two nerdy college guys helping an attractive college girl is extremely easy to swallow."

Jason added, "And it puts us in the background rather than being out front. Having two guys going around with metal detectors would make the locals nervous. It's much different when you have a good looking young girl doing the looking with two seemingly lovesick guys helping. It works. It's a good cover."

Ella, a bit embarrassed, said, "Well, I'm glad you two geeks think I'm attractive, and I can get used to having you at my 'beck and call' for whatever my little ole' heart desires."

The guys laughed and Jason vowed, "Yes, my lady. Just tell us what dragons you want slayed."

Kole, down on one knee, joined in. "We shall bring you one of the dragon's heads to show our devotion."

"Okay, Okay," responded Ella. "I know my limits. But I like the idea."

Kole was back in his professorial role. "Now that we have that settled, let's talk about equipment."

CHAPTER 15

Equipment

Placed in charge of planning, Kole was instructing the others. "We need to bring our laptops, of course. Also, we need our metal detectors to support our cover story. However, the fact is they are useless when it comes to searching for the gold. That's because the tunnel where the Confederates buried the gold is probably seventy or eighty feet underground. The stuff Jason and I have only looks a couple of feet below the surface. So, we need special equipment. And I found it! It is a DJI Phantom 4 drone with a DroneRover sensor attachment. The drone can scan an area for treasure and find a single bar of gold buried up to eighty feet below the surface. This drone can find a big cache, like the one we are looking for, as deep as a hundred or more feet underground. And the beauty of it is we can do our search on the sly while most people are sound asleep. The drone's screen displays a satellite map. We highlight the area we want to search and press the 'Go' button. That's all there is to it. The Phantom does the rest automatically. And it's smart—dodging obstacles and marking its finds with GPS coordinates."

Jason was shaking his head in a mixture of questioning and disbelief. "That is amazing! I had no idea that drone technology was that advanced. But it must cost a fortune. How can we afford this? How much does the drone cost?"

"No worries. The Phantom 4 is not going to cost us anything. In fact, I already have it. All we have to do is return the equipment in one piece. So do not break it!"

"How?" asked Ella. "How do you get stuff like this without our having to pay for it?"

"Let's just say I know somebody who knows somebody and leave it at that."

Jason still wasn't sure about the idea of free, 'borrowed,' equipment, especially expensive equipment. "Kole, tell me we aren't about to do something illegal."

"No, nothing like that. Everything is okay. It's perfectly legal, but ours is not the kind of deal that my source wants others to know about. Also, I have something else to help us. It's a Minelab GPZ 7000. This is a hand-held extreme depth detector that is tuned for maximum gold sensitivity and has an integrated GPS. Once the drone has given us its GPS coordinates, we can use the Minelab to get on top of the gold."

Worried, Ella wasn't convinced. "You make it sound so simple. But what happens if we can't dig it out. You know, maybe a building is on top of it, or it is in the middle of a road or somewhere else that we can't get to?"

"Then we go to Plan B."

CHAPTER 16

Plan B

"What is Plan B?" groaned Jason wearily.

"We find what is left of the tunnel. Get inside and dig our way through the explosion debris until we get to the point where General Welch and his men left the gold."

"Okay, Genius," exclaimed Jason. "I suspect you already have something that will find the tunnel for us."

Kole pulled out what looked like an iWatch. "This is not something that is commercially available. I was able to borrow this prototype. It's a gravity sensor. It is so sensitive that it can detect one-part-per-billion changes in Earth's gravitational field. In simple terms, there will be a minuscule change in gravity if we walk across a tunnel. Although the difference is tiny, the tunnel causes an abrupt change in the gravitational pull of the earth at that point. You wear it like a watch. The sensor will let us know when we are on top of a remnant of the original tunnel by a slight vibration or an audible buzzing sound. The watch's display, its face, indicates the width and the depth of the tunnel's ceiling and floor."

"Now you are scaring me again." Jason found the iWatch thing on top of all the other exotic equipment hard to take. "No ordinary mortal can come up with all this stuff. Especially this gravity sensor gismo thing. This is spy stuff—like gadgets from a 007 movie!"

Ella said, "Me too, Kole. How do you do it?"

"Come on guys. There is nothing sinister here. I know some geniuses who work for Elon Musk. And on the side, they have been working on this device competing for a DARPA grant."

"What is DARPA?" asked Ella.

"DARPA is an acronym for the Defense Advanced Research Projects Agency. The agency identifies military re-lated problems and then challenges the commercial world, or individuals, to produce a solution. Sometimes, it's a monetary reward after the fact, or it is a front-end monetary grant to develop and refine a proposed solution. The military has become concerned about subterranean battlegrounds. They need the ability to pursue and fight an enemy that has taken to the underground—tunnels or caves. My Elon Musk friends are competing for the tunnel identification grant. All the USA has right now to do the job is ground-penetrating radar. That is cumbersome and the results are too subjective. The military wants a small, simple device that can be widely deployed."

Jason rolled his eyes as he sputtered, "How do you know all this stuff?"

"I can't help it; my family has a lot of connections with the military. They talk. I listen."

"Okay," responded Jason. "But why would those geniuses of yours let you have their watch?"

"They are friends of the family and I convinced them that we would be a good field test for them. They need a record of successes to support their grant request."

Accepting his explanation, Jason said, "Okay dude, but you've got to admit this is far out. This family of yours has got to be something else, man. Where are you from, anyway?"

"Well, it's a big family. We're from all over."

"Europe, the UK?" Jason asked.

"Some, I moved around a lot."

Sensing Kole's reluctance to talk about his past, Jason let it drop. "Kole, I can only say, we are damn lucky to have you as our partner."

Kole with a sly smile said, "Forget about it," in his best New Jersey mobster accent.

"There you go scaring me again," joked Jason. "Don't do that!"

"Okay, I won't pull any more rabbits out of the hat."

Ella interjected, "Don't be too quick to stop with the magic tricks. We may need one more."

"What's that?"

"The internet, how do we get connected? We don't want to use any shared networks like hotels have."

"No problem! I have it covered. You haven't noticed but here at your place Ella, our laptops are connected to Starlink. So, we will still have our internet connection even in Asheville."

"Okay, now you have done it!" scolded Jason. "Now you are scaring me big time! I keep up with Starlink availability, and it is not available below forty-five degrees latitude."

"Honestly, Jason, it is okay," protested Kole. "Starlink is working toward full U.S. coverage. While there is no commercially available access in our area right now, the area is in beta testing. My Musk contacts gave me their beta access code. We are just getting advance access by linking to pre-paratorily placed Starlink satellites in fixed orbit."

"Okay, you just happened to know somebody who knows somebody, right?"

"Right."

"Geez, in addition to knowing important somebodies and really big words, you'll be walking on water next."

It was the week before fall break, and it had been a busy one. After determining that the strip of Buncombe Turnpike that ran through town was now called Broadway, the students estimated that the tunnel must have started near what is now South Pack Square between where Broadway is crossed by Patton and College Streets and that according to the diary, it ran for approximately three hundred fifty-two steps. They decided that James Donelson Walker's stride would approximate a yard more or less. So, the tunnel would have continued from its beginning at Pack Square for one thousand sixty-six feet. They drew a line for their estimate of the tunnel's position on a city map and realized that the tunnel would have terminated at the spot now occupied by Asheville's Masonic Lodge.

That was not the worst of their findings. Their estimated route of the tunnel now ran under an almost continuous row of commercial buildings in the heart of Asheville's business district. It was looking increasingly like they would have to go to Plan B.

They also did more research on Corporal Walker, his mother, and their Maple Street address. Mrs. Walker was a teacher. She taught English and Latin which, they thought accounted for her son's penmanship. Corporal Walker returned from the war and lived with his mother until his death from cholera in 1868. There was nothing to indicate that he had made any attempt to recover the gold.

As for General George Andrew Welch, after hiding the gold in Asheville and telling his men to scatter, he had continued to travel north with the wagon. It was a diversion to fool the Union troops into continuing to follow him not realizing that his men and the gold remained in Asheville. Within the year, he was killed in a bar fight in Benezette, Pennsylvania near the community of Dents Run. Their research had also disclosed that after fleeing Asheville, he became a member of a secret society called the Knights of the Golden Circle or KGC. The KGC believed the South would rise again, and they began a campaign to accumulate wealth including gold and other valuables which they hid for financing the return of the South when the time was right. To that end, Welch traveled the country stealing from anyone without regard to their political leanings. His escapades had only just begun when he met his end. Given his activities and untimely death, Jason and team concluded he had not had time to make any effort to recover the cache of Atlanta gold.

The three now felt confident that they knew where the gold was hidden and that the treasure was still there. They were not so confident that they could get to the stolen shipment. But they all agreed it was too big of a prize not to go for it.

CHAPTER 17

Civil War 101

By the middle of October, the three had packed the equipment and enough clothes for a week. They left for Applewood Manor early in the morning.

After traveling for a while, Ella suggested that she update the guys on the Civil War. "Given our cover story dealing with Civil War prisons and since we are going to be in Asheville, supposedly investigating the city's involvement in the War, I thought I needed to refresh my memory about it. So, I've been doing some reading. If you want, I can fill you in as to what I've learned."

Jason quickly agreed. "Good idea, I can use a refresher course and your lesson will make the drive go faster."

Kole teased, "So, Professor Ella Blakeford give us the university course, U.S. Civil War 101."

Ella laughed. "I'll do my best, but it won't qualify for college credit. I will just hit the high spots concentrating on those areas most important for us.

"Well, South Carolina started things off immediately after Lincoln was elected in January 1861 by calling for a state

67

convention to remove itself from the United States. The rest of the southern states followed suit—Florida, Mississippi, Georgia, Alabama, Louisiana, Texas, then finally, Virginia, Arkansas, Tennessee, and North Carolina followed. They formed the Confederate States of America or CSA.

"The official start of the War, which would become the bloodiest in our history, was in April of 1861 with the CSA's victory against the Union at Fort Sumter in South Carolina. It ended on April 9, 1865 on the courthouse steps of Appomattox Station, Virginia when General Robert E. Lee surrendered to General Ulysses S. Grant.

"At the beginning of the War, both sides were not prepared for the tremendous logistical challenges of feeding and clothing their men. And that challenge was even greater when it came to their prisoners of war. Both sides had agreed that enemy prisoners should be treated humanely, and both sides tried to comply. Unfortunately, both sides failed miserably. The infrastructure to manage the transportation, care, and guarding of prisoners was nonexistent, and 'make do' arrangements were the order of the day. And, of course, there was only so much to go around. So, the needs of the prisoners took second place when it came to resources—including food.

"Four million men fought in the Civil War—about two million on each side. Ten percent of those, or four hundred thousand men, became prisoners. And tragically around sixty thousand of those soldiers died in prison. They died from ill treatment of wounds, from illnesses arising from dismal sanitary conditions, from contaminated food and water, and from a lack of adequate clothing and shelter. Medical care was non-existent in many prisons and inadequate in the others. Both North and South were plagued by mismanagement and for the South a debilitating lack of resources."

Jason interrupted Ella's lecture. "We are now passing Cookeville, which, you might not know, is about eleven miles from the midpoint between Nashville and Knoxville. In about ten more minutes, we will drive past the town of Pinhook which is the exactly the midpoint. That means, if we don't stop, we will reach Knoxville in exactly one hour and twenty-six minutes."

Kole couldn't help himself. "Well, Ella, it seems we have another learned instructor in our midst. Thank you, Professor McConnell, for the geography lesson and travel report."

"Hey man, I'm only trying to keep you guys posted on our progress."

"And we greatly appreciate it," replied Kole with a laugh.

"As you should. And as one learned professor to another, please continue, Miss Blakeford."

The break gave Ella the chance to catch her breath and drink some of her water. "Well, since we are talking about Tennessee, did you know we were one of the earliest targets for the Union army? That was because of the importance of our rail system. By the summer of 1863, Tennessee was completely under occupation by the Union army.

"Initially, Union authorities pursued a lenient occupation policy in the hope of winning over secessionist citizens. That didn't work. People remained hostile, defiant, and fought back. So, their treatment of people in the South changed. New policies included seizure and destruction of private property, imprisonment, or banishment of those who refused to take an oath of allegiance to the Union, and, of course, freeing slaves. That change from lenient to harsh policies is said to have culminated in General William T. Sherman's burning of Atlanta and his march to the sea.

"Moving on to North Carolina, the Battle of Asheville in 1865 was just before Corporal Walker and General Welch arrived with the gold. People say it would be better described as the non-battle of Asheville. Asheville was an important Confederate center with military training camps and an armory where the South was manufacturing Enfield type rifles. It was also well fortified, protected by CSA troops and its canons on Battery Hill in the center of town. The South had dug battlements across areas where they thought the Union army would attack. But the attack never happened. Union Colonel Isaac M. Kirby had been ordered to capture the city but only if he could do so without serious losses. Kirby's advance was met by a group of civilians on the out-skirts of the city. Coming under fire, Colonel Kirby decided to bypass Asheville and move on to easier targets. After that, the cannons and CSA troops stationed in Asheville were withdrawn to redeploy elsewhere in support of other North Carolina cities." Ella stopped, took another drink from her water bottle, and said, "Guys, I think that concludes the Civil War 101. Maybe I'll do the Civil War 201 version later. Right now, I'm going close my eyes and try to relax for a while."

"Good idea," Jason replied. "This is going to be a long day."

Kole added. "Speaking of a long day, do you want me to give you a break?"

"Do you mean drive?"

"Right, I hate to let you do all the work on this trip."

Jason laughed. "Thanks just the same, buddy, but you might put us on the wrong side of the road."

"You've got it backwards, mate. It's you Yankees that drive on the wrong side."

Ella interrupted their banter. "Guys, guys—some other time, please. I'm trying to sleep."

Kole replied, "Yes, my lady, your wish is our command."

"Ditto" added Jason. "And thanks for the offer, Kole. Maybe later."

For a while they drove in silence. Then Jason announced, "We are coming up on a rest stop. This is the last rest stop on this side of Asheville. Next, we enter the mountains. Let's stretch our legs and take advantage of the facilities. Next stop is the Applewood Manor."

As they continued their trip, the world outside the SUV is what held their attention. The mid-October drive from Knoxville to Asheville was an explosion of fall colors. The mountains contain one of highest diversity of deciduous trees anywhere in the world with every species having its own characteristic color. That diversity combined with the continuous change in altitude provided a kaleidoscope of brown, yellow, orange, red, purple, and some lingering green. Fall wildflowers covered the ground with their own blanket of color. They stopped along the route several times exiting just to reach an overlook where they could soak up spectacular views and enjoy the cool mountain air. As they stood at the last overlook, Ella breathed a relaxing sigh. She whispered, "I just wasn't expecting this! Even if we never find our gold treasure, this gorgeous day and the fall colors make it the best break, spring or fall, I have ever had!"

As they drove into the city, Kole asked that he be dropped off near the Grove Arcade building so he could get the lay of the land and brief the others in a couple of hours.

The Arcade in the center of downtown Asheville is the in place where tourists and locals go to shop and eat. The idea for the Arcade came from E.W. Grove. He was a self-made millionaire who moved to Asheville in 1910 and began plans in 1920 to build the Arcade to enliven the downtown of the city he had come to love. He conceived of the Arcade as an elegant building that would be a new kind of retail center—in a sense, he invented the mall. Grove died in 1927 prior to its completion. Designed by architect, Charles N. Parker, the Arcade is one of North Carolina's most historic and beautiful commercial buildings. Outside, the portico is where you'll find local farmers and craftspeople selling their wares. There are outdoor sidewalk pet-friendly restaurants. The inside includes prime evening dining spots along with upscale shops and galleries.

Kole's request seemed like a good move. One that would save time—and one person canvassing the area had the advantage of not drawing unwanted attention. They stopped at the Arcade long enough for Kole to jump out and with his agreement that he would also walk to Applewood Manor to check out that route.

After dropping off Kole, Ella and Jason drove on to Applewood Manor at 62 Cumberland Circle. They paid little attention to the exterior of inn as they arrived. They hadn't thought about it earlier—that they were checking in as a couple. This was something that they had never done before with anyone. Now they were very nervous about the appearance of it. Frankly, they wished Kole was with them—three was less intimate appearing. Ella spent the time pretending to look at the art on display. In truth, she was trying to mentally will herself elsewhere. Jason pretended to be nonchalant, but his hand trembled as he fumbled to give his credit card to the smiling innkeeper. As she handed him a key, she said, "We have the perfect place for you. I'm sure you will enjoy our roomy Cortland Cottage." With that, the check-in was quickly completed . Before leaving the reception area, Jason did manage to explain that a friend of theirs, also on fall break, might join them. The innkeeper advised that the addition would be okay, but Jason thought she looked like she didn't really believe him. He couldn't even remember her name even thought she had been friendly and introduced herself.

Ella and Jason thought they were lucky to get the Cortland Cottage, which was separated from the main house with its own parking area. They learned later that the choice wasn't pure luck. The Cortland is considered Applewood's Honeymoon Cottage, and both had a good laugh.

The registration taken care of, Jason and Ella unloaded everything from the car, and while waiting for Kole, they set up the computers and organized their supplies and tools. They were all set—anxious to begin the search for their buried treasure.

After finishing his reconnaissance of the suspected route of the tunnel, Kole headed for the bed and breakfast inn, on foot as promised. He remembered that it was only a short walk, and within just ten minutes, his walk had taken him to Montford Avenue. He entered the Montford Historic District, where the tree-lined streets play host to an eclectic variety of architectural influences reflecting the cosmopolitan character of Asheville during the turn of the 20th century. The styles vary from Victorian, Queen Anne, and

Craftsman to Neoclassical and Colonial Revival. Kole even passed one home that looked like a castle. He was fascinated by the thought that this unique neighborhood was so close to the busy center of the city. He knew from the inn's website that the area included more than 600 homes built between 1890 and 1920 and they were all on the National Historic Register. Many of the residences had been restored in recent years, and some like Applewood Manor were converted to bed and breakfast inns. After another fifteen minutes or so, he arrived at a small neighborhood grocery store at the corner of Montford Avenue and Cullowhee Street. The store was pie-shaped because between Montford and Cullowhee is Soco Steet which slices diagonally between the two providing a direct path to Cumberland Circle. Once on Cumberland Circle, it would be less than a quarter of a mile to Applewood Manor. Kole decided to do a little shopping in the grocery store before joining Ella and Jason at the inn.

CHAPTER 18

Cottage Lunch

Kole arrived with his purchases from the small grocery store—a liter of Mountain Dew, a family size bag of Doritos, a wedge of Comte cheese, a baguette, and for himself a six pack of Hi-Wire Lager, one of Asheville's popular craft beers. Jason and Ella were glad see Kole, but their immediate attention was on the food. The baguette was sliced, and they hungrily went for the bread and cheese lunch. They would be working tonight and not taking advantage of the plethora of restaurants in Asheville.

While Jason and Ella snacked on chips and drank Mountain Dew, Kole, who was a couple of years older, opened one of the Hi-Wire beers and began telling them about his casing efforts. "I am not sure our drone can do much for us. It's wall to wall commercial buildings along what we think is the tunnel's path. However, there are some intervening parking lots and patches of terra firma—small, landscaped areas. But we could get lucky, especially when the parking areas are empty late at night or early morning. I can tell you that I was wearing the gravity instrument and I did pick up indications of underground voids between sixty and eighty feet below the surface. These were in areas I could walk over including some small passages between buildings and one location near the South Pack Square. I did not feel comfortable staying long enough to get full measurements without looking suspicious. Nevertheless, the readings I did get confirm that a tunnel is there, and our calculations are right on target."

Kole could sense the complex feelings of his team-mates—excitement combined with a concern that it could all go wrong.

Jason asked, "What are our next steps?"

"We let our bird loose tonight. We may not get anything, but I say the sooner we find out the better—let's get it over with. If the drone cannot get the job done, we will switch to our other boots-on-the-ground tools including the Minelab GPZ 7000 handheld deep detector."

Ella spoke up. "When do we do it and do we fly the drone from here?"

"I suggest about three in the morning. Even the night owls should be gone by that time and the early risers will be in the shower, if awake at all. On my way back from town, I checked out the greenfields around this place. There is an open field behind Applewood's patio landscaping, that's perfect—plenty of space and secluded.

Chapter 19

Drone

Before sunup, the three quietly left the Cortland Cottage at two fifteen. It was a cold cloudless night, and the moon was lighting their way. Every step in the gravel and through the leaves seemed to be amplified a hundred times. Although the lights were out in the inn and most of the neighboring houses, Ella was tense. She whispered, "What if someone sees us?" Jason reminded her, "We stick to our cover story. We are surveying the area to find evidence of Asheville's involvement in the Civil War and the best time for flying our drone is when the area is free from people and cars."

The drone weighed only about five pounds with the DroneRover attachment but despite its light weight, hauling the thing was not that easy. The four propellers made holding the Phantom 4 difficult. Kole took the job of transporting the drone and Jason had the control unit. Ella carried a small duffel bag with water, blanket, and a few other items in case they were needed.

They crossed Applewood Manor's large patio and took a stone walkway that led them through its heavy landscaping to an open field. It was the perfect spot to launch the drone. Jason and Kole went back to the Manor's patio and borrowed a bistro table and chair. The table was for the small laptop-like control unit and the chair was for Kole to use as the drone's operator. Ella spread out the blanket on the grass, but neither she nor Jason sat. They stood behind Kole, looking over his shoulders at the screen of the Phantom's control computer.

At three o'clock the drone rose vertically until the Phantom 4 was a mere dot against the moonlit sky. Then under Kole's control, it headed southeast to Pack Square to begin its northwesterly search along Broadway. Arriving at the starting point for the search, Kole activated the DroneRover attachment. The Phantom 4 drone began moving slowly along its search area. Ella silently cheered in excitement as the first images appeared. Excitement turned to astonishment as she and the others viewed the displayed skeletons of buildings. The bones were steel beams, water pipes, and electrical conduits. In some buildings the clutter of infrastructure was so dense that the subterranean view was totally obscured. Other buildings gave the drone a clear view of what was under them—mainly sewers and more water pipes plus various kinds of buried debris.

The control unit's display was devoted largely to visual images, but on the right side of the control computer, numerical data was being displayed—GPS coordinates and numbers, one of which seemed to change continually but was repeating often. Pointing to the changing numbers, Ella asked, "What do those numbers mean?"

Kole explained without looking up. "That is the density of the material in the crosshair on the view screen. The numbers represent grams per cubic centimeters. We found iron, copper, some lead, and other common building materials. But what we are looking for is 19.32—that's the density of gold."

As the drone worked its way slowly down the search area, Kole had the Phantom 4 hover above each building to peer down through the structure's skeleton searching eighty feet below ground for the gold. By four that morning, the drone reached the Masonic Lodge and the end of the search area. The computer density instrument display indicated the presence of small amounts of gold, silver, and platinum, but all of it was in the building's structure and what appeared be a basement but nothing in the subterranean.

Jason asked, "Kole, do you know the distance from our beginning point?"

"Yes, we have gone about three hundred eighty yards."

"Isn't that beyond our estimates of the point where the gold should be?"

"Yeah, by about thirty yards. Since our estimate was just that, an estimate, I thought I would have the drone look a little further."

"Let's try flying it back by those thirty yards and hovering for another look. Where does that put us?"

Kole did so and said, "Okay, we are exactly at three hundred fifty two yards from our estimate of the tunnel's beginning. Visually, we are on the beginning edge of the Masonic Lodge parking lot."

"Anything down there?"

Kole studied the screen. "I'm getting something. Just hold on for second." He had the DroneRover drill deeper into the subterranean passing the eighty foot depth level. "We are entering a void—the tunnel, I think." After a minute he said, "It's registering 7.874. That's iron and a hell of a lot of it."

"What do you think that means?" asked Jason.

"It means there is a lot of iron where it shouldn't be and where the gold should be."

All three stared at the control unit. Finally, Jason asked, "Anyone want to hazard a guess?"

Ella said, "Isn't that what the Confederates used to make their cannon balls?"

"Of course, you're right!" Jason shouted slapping his head. "I think that's exactly what they hid there, cannon balls, instead of the gold."

Kole added, "Or that is what someone put there after taking the gold."

It would be light soon, and cars and trucks were beginning to arrive in the city as early shift workers began their workday. There was nothing to do but recover the drone, take the table and chair back to the patio before they were missed, and return to their cottage to ponder what they did wrong, if anything. The alternative was to decide that there is no gold. The diary was just a make-believe story, or someone had gotten to it first!

CHAPTER 20

Missing

Kole and Ella were rather down as they returned to the cottage. But not Jason, the gambler. In his book, tomorrow was always another day and another chance to find their gold. "Guys, that gold is still out there. We need to be clear-headed—go back to the beginning, go over everything to see what we have missed. We can't do that in the condition we are in right now. We need food and sleep. It's already five-thirty, still too early for breakfast—so take a break, a nap if you can, and plan on going to the main house about seven for breakfast. Then we'll come back to the cottage and crash for three or four hours."

A little before seven as they left the cottage for breakfast, Ella said, "I am starving." Then with a little chuckle she added, "I always eat when I'm depressed."

Kole added, "What I need for once is a strong cup of brew."

As the three walked to the Manor, they couldn't help feeling that they were stepping back in time. The 1912 home turned bed and breakfast is an early New England style colonial structure of apple-red cedar siding with all white porches and trim work. They climbed up the steps to its pediment entrance and as they opened the door, they were greeted by three very active French Bulldogs. Of course, that stopped them in their tracks until they and the dogs were acquainted. Robin, the innkeeper, came to the rescue. "Good morning. I see you have met Applewood's mascots. The cream one is Pearl, and the two brindles, the dark ones, are Cleo and Ziggy."

Ella said, "They are so cute. I want to take them back to the cottage with me."

Robin laughed, "I'm afraid you would have to get in line."

Kole interrupted, "I don't know what's cooking, but the aroma alone is awesome. Whatever that is, it's calling my name."

The dogs went on their way and Robin led them to their table. If they were expecting ham and eggs, they were in for a surprise. Breakfast at Applewood Manor is never that simple. That day's breakfast was a polenta bake with sausage from the nearby Hickory Nut Farm and a mixed green salad with toasted almonds and goat cheese, and of course, Robin's homemade bread right out of the oven!

They returned to the cottage no longer hungry but still weary. While their gourmet breakfast couldn't reverse Kole's and Ella's disappointment over the drone results, the dining room experience did lift them out of the doldrums. As Jason would say, tomorrow is another day to search for the gold. All three found a spot to finally rest.

***

At one in the afternoon, after about five hours of shuteye, Jason and Ella were up and were wondering where Kole was. Then Ella pointed to the new groceries on the table and Jason said, "I guess Kole got up earlier and went back to the store."

Ella had moved to the table. "He brought lunch—cold cuts, more cheese, apples, a liter of Diet Coke and one of Sprite. And there are rolls that look they came from a local bakery. But where is he now?"

Jason helped himself to the Diet Coke. "He must have gone out for something. I'll bet he is walking the search area with his gravity watch. But there is no reason to wait. Let's eat."

Neither he nor Ella wasted anymore time thinking about the missing Kole. As they ate, Ella thought everything tasted better in Asheville. She wondered if it was just the mountain air, or did locally grown and raised really make that much of a difference?

After their lunch, they found Kole's note: "Enjoy lunch on me. I decided to walk the search area again. I've taken the gravity device to see if I detect any other tunnels or underground vaults. Will check back later."

"There you go. I was right as usual," joked Jason.

As things turned out there was a problem after all. And the problem was a big one. Kole did not return that day, that night, or even the next day.

When Kole dropped off the groceries, he found his two companions still asleep, so he decided to go back to town with the gravity watch. Maybe there were other tunnels nearby or spurs off of their targeted tunnel where the gold was really buried. The gravity watch would find them and then they could use the drone or the deep search detectors to determine if they held gold. He left the cottage and headed for town. He took the secluded crossover road from Cumberland Circle to Montford Avenue. He thought he was the only person on the sidewalk but just as he was approaching the corner store, he noticed that someone was walking behind him—a large man in a suit. He had seen a lot of walkers and bike riders around Montford so another walker wouldn't have been unusual, but someone in a suit and tie, no! Just as that thought formed in his mind, the man bumped him from behind, and he felt a sting in the back of his neck.

That was the last thing he remembered until the car. He was in a car—in the back seat lying on his side. A plastic tie was around his wrists, and though he couldn't see it, apparently there was another tie around his ankles because he couldn't separate his legs. He wanted to ask what was going on but there was tape over his mouth. His eyes were uncovered but of little use because he could not see out the windows of the car. As his head cleared, he realized that he was being kidnapped and he tried to think what to do, but he couldn't. His head hurt and his thinking was still foggy. He finally decided that he should try to remember where he was being taken.

They were clearly on a winding road. He could feel the car sway as it took one curve after another. He could see the gravity watch. It showed an increase in gravitational pull. They had to still be in the mountains, but they were declining in altitude—going down.

There was a change. Now the road was smooth—probably paved, no bumps or potholes. The car stopped and for the first time, there was the noise of other cars and the sound of people talking, but Kole couldn't make out what they were saying. We must be at a traffic light in a town of some kind he thought. The car started, turned left and the road became rough—gravel, and even more twisting than before. Now the elevation was increasing. The car was going much slower and seemed labored, going up a steep hill. He thought they were probably on a driveway but longer and with sharp turns.

The car finally came to stop. Kole's door opened and he remembered seeing a rustic cabin just before he felt a new sting on the back of his neck.

When Kole had not returned to the cottage by evening, Jason and Ella were past worrying. They were in full-blown panic mode! They retraced the steps they thought he would have taken to return to town. They walked up and down Broadway looking for Kole. They expanded their search to side streets and shops. They checked hospitals for anyone admitted that matched Kole's description. But they found nothing—no Kole and no one who had seen him. Finally, Jason did the last thing he wanted to do. He called the police to report a missing person.

CHAPTER 21

The Police

The police responded quickly to Jason's phone call. They had been friendly and seemed genuinely concerned over Kole's disappearance. The officers knew the owners of Applewood Manor and being a guest of the B&B seemed to carry a lot of weight. When they left, they had said, "We're on it. We will get back with you as soon as we know something." Now the police were back. This time, they weren't friendly, and their concern had been replaced with a strictly business attitude.

Jason tried to explain. "Officer, I'll tell you again, Kole said his last name was impossible to pronounce. He mumbled something once, but neither of us can remember it. Kole didn't seem to want to go into it, and we didn't care."

"I'm sorry, Mr. McConnell. We can't help you. You can't even tell me the missing man's full name. And we checked with the University. They have no one enrolled at Belmont with Kole as either their first or last name. Even the innkeeper at Applewood Manor says no one by that name is registered. It seems to me that you and your friend are playing some sort of game. That is called wasting police time, and I can book you for that. It is a misdemeanor here in Asheville."

"Officer, Kole is a good friend," pleaded Jason. "None of this makes any sense. Miss Blakeford will vouch for what I'm saying. Kole was here with us on fall break. We were helping Ella, Miss Blakeford, with her Civil War project."

"Well now, we may have grown up in these mountains, but that doesn't make us stupid. We checked your story. And the University says Miss Blakeford has not been assigned anything having to do with Asheville or the Civil War. So, I am going to go back to my cruiser and then back to the station. If I hear anything else from you about this missing person, you will spend the rest of your fall break in our city jail! Is that clear?"

Jason and Ella were dumbfounded. And at a loss as to what to do next. Ella began crying. "What do you think has happened to him?"

"Ella, I don't know what to think. But what about the fact that neither you nor I really know anything about Kole. How did he get all the equipment—drones, detectors, computers, satellite hookups, and what about that gravity watch? We don't even know his last name! Maybe Kole is even an alias. You remember how he had us let him out downtown while we registered at Applewood. He didn't want to register, did he? I can't remember ever seeing him use a credit card. And the phone thing. Why didn't he want to have a cellphone? We do not have anything to prove he ever existed. This is scary. We need help!"

Ella agreed regaining her composure. "Yeah, it is frightening. What can we do?"

CHAPTER 22

The Cavalry

"Mr. Rollins this is Jennifer McConnell. I hope you remember me."

"Yes, of course I do Jen. Forget the mister. Call me Mark. You are one of my most loyal members. I remember welcoming you in 2004 when we first opened the doors of the Women's Health Club. That makes you a founding member!"

"I cannot believe that was eighteen years ago and that means I am eighteen years older. You know Mark, time moves too fast these days. I wish it would slow down."

"I know what you mean, but I don't think you called me to go over old times. What can I do for you?"

"It's my son, Jason McConnell. He is a sophomore at Belmont University. He and two of his friends (one is a girl) went to Asheville for their fall break. Jason called me early this morning quite shook up. I would not bother you except I have never seen my son afraid of anything. And the boy sounded scared out of his mind. It seems one of the three has gone missing. According to Jason, the police are not helping to find their friend. The police seem to think that Jason and the girl with him are just making the missing person thing up—like a game. My son is extremely self-reliant. For him to cry out to me for help means he must be involved in something that is serious—even dangerous. Could you call him? See if you can figure out what is going on and either help them or point Jason and the girl to someone who can?"

"You said they are in Asheville, North Carolina?"

"Yes, a bed and breakfast inn by the name of Applewood Manor. I really do not understand clearly what they are doing there. I don't remember Asheville being high on the list of college break locations. My motherly instinct tells me they are up to something. I just don't know what that something is."

"Jen, I'll do better than call. I will be there in four or five hours. Call your son and tell him to write down everything he can think of that might help me find his friend."

After being thanked profusely, Mark Rollins ended the call and immediately buzzed Shannon Nelson. Shannon is his nature-loving receptionist who is always involved in some cause orientated effort to save the environment or its animal inhabitants. "Shannon, phone the folks at Stratos Jet Charter and have them arrange for a plane. I want to go to Asheville, North Carolina. I will be at their executive lounge within two hours, so have the plane and pilot ready to go."

The next call was to the first number on his phone's favorites list, his wife Sarah Rollins. "Hi Sarah."

"Hi yourself." Sarah continued teasingly, "Usually when you call me this soon after going to the office, it isn't just because you want to hear the sound of my voice."

"Nope, but I'm afraid you're right as usual. I need to make a trip to Asheville for a few days. There is a problem

90

involving the son of one of the WH Club's members. I hope that won't screw up any plans."

Sarah is someone who is always interested and concerned about others, particularly her friends and their children. So she immediately asked, "Who are we talking about, and do you know what the problem is?"

"It's about Jason McConnell, Jennifer's son. Apparently, a friend he was traveling with has disappeared. I'll have Tony go with me."

"Oh no! Of course, you must go. Don't worry about me. I will be fine."

Then he called Tony Caruso. Tony is best described as Rollins' driver and bodyguard although the bodyguard designation does not appear anywhere in the employment records at the Woman's Health Club. "Tony, how would you like to make a trip to Asheville with me. Hopefully, it will be a fast turnaround, but you and I should be prepared to stay for a few days." After driving Rollins to his office that morning, Tony had returned to his apartment over the carriage house. The carriage house was an addition to the Rollins family home to house golfcarts used to navigate the grounds of what is referred to by the locals as the Rollins Compound. It turned out to be a handy solution for keeping Tony close by for security purposes. "Get my bag from Sarah and meet me at the WH Club in an hour."

Next, Rollins called Bryan Gray, the WH Club's Chief Information Officer. Rollins prefers to call him the head of his Brain Trust. "Bryan, the son of one of our members is on fall break in Asheville, North Carolina and has run into some trouble. I am flying to Asheville to see if we can do anything to help. There is a missing person involved so I wanted to give you a heads up. I may need the Brain Trust. I will call you with specifics when I know more."

"Roger, Chief, we will be on standby."

He made one final call before meeting Tony for the drive to the private air service. It was to Meg Scott, Rollins' married daughter and the manager of the WH Club. "Meg, you will be on your own for a couple of days. I have to go to Asheville. If you need me, you know how to get touch."

"I have it, Dad. There is nothing in the works that should require your involvement—no unhappy members and no trainers with a domestic crisis. You take care and I'll check on Mother in case she needs anything."

Mark walked out the back door of the WH Club and climbed into the back seat his Lexus, christened Black Beauty by the Brain Trust geeks who had hardened the LS 460 with defensive measures including bulletproofing. And they added one or two offensive assets that are probably illegal. The vehicle also functions as a mobile office with full communications capabilities. Why does Mark Rollins require a combination driver-bodyguard and a car that has been turned into a tank on wheels? It seems he cannot stay away from other people's problems. Some of which eventually turn into dangerous ones.

CHAPTER 23

Snatched

When Kole woke up, he was alone seated in a wooden chair in an otherwise empty log cabin room with his ankle chained to an eye bolt in a ceiling rafter. All he could think of was a dog. He was chained like a dog. The chain was long enough that he could move around the room but not reach the door and the room's one window. He could reach the bathroom next to his chair.

He shouted, "Is anyone here?" When there was no answer, he screamed HELP over and over until the door opened and a big man, the man who had been on the sidewalk behind him, came into the room.

"I see you are awake," the man chuckled.

Kole erupted, "What is all this? Who the hell are you and why—why am I here? Why the chain?"

"Just take it easy and everything will be okay."

"Bollocks. That is complete bollocks!" snapped Kole. "None of this is okay."

"Look, fellow, you only have two choices. You can cooperate and get out of that chain and back to your two friends, or you can keep screaming at me and find yourself back in the Czech Republic."

Kole was shocked and the look on his face showed it. Who was this guy he thought. And how did he know about the Czech Republic?

"Yes, that's right, kid. We know who you are—Kole Mrázek. You are the grandson of the new Boss's predecessor, good old Francis. And he is currently swimming with the fishes along with most of your family. Tell us what you're doing in Asheville with all that exotic equipment, or you can play hardball and get shipped back to the shithole country you came from. And you and I both know you would not last twenty-four hours if the new Czech Godfather found out you were still alive."

Kole shouted at the man, "What equipment?" But he was thinking—how did he know about the equipment or, for that matter, about me?

"Mrázek, you got it all wrong. I ask the questions—you answer the questions! You got that?"

Kole replied slowly with clinched teeth. "I am not telling you anything until I know who you are!"

"Take a guess, kid!"

"Let me see. I've got it. You're either some loser out for kicks or you are going to hold me for ransom. If that's it, you are in for a big disappointment—maybe my friends can raise a dollar and a half between them!"

"Well, funny man, here are my FBI credentials. We finally pegged you when your facial image pinged in our D.C. headquarters. The FBI has its own cameras on the southern border. We know you were a gotaway. The border guys were just too busy to run after your ass. So, you think that since you have your feet on our soil, the glowing City on the Hill, that you are home free. Well, you are wrong. Remember that the FBI can deport you and send you right back to your lousy homeland. That's right. We can put you on a plane tonight and send you back where there are people who want you erased for good. The surprising thing is you would have qualified for asylum, if you had turned yourself in at the border and asked for it. Now that we have an understanding, Kole Mrázek, what I want to know is what was in that book?"

Kole sat up straighter. He could not believe the question. "What book are you talking about?"

"Did you know that we have people who do nothing but watch security camera videos. They watch for hours and hours, day after day, just looking for that one thing the subject doesn't want us to see. We saw your friend absconding with the book!"

"How?" asked Kole "How could you possibly know that!"

"The FBI is very thorough. When we caught you in our camera lens, we started backtracking on you and your friends. We got hold of the library security camera recording, and our people watched until they saw your buddy, Jason Stewart McConnell. We watched him examine the book, study its contents, and then instead of recording it in the library's database, he put it in his backpack and hurried out to meet you and Ms. Ella Blakeford in the University's dining hall. Yeah, that's right! We even looked at the dining hall's security archives, too. The agency leaves no stone unturned."

"I really don't understand what is going on here." Kole asked, "So, are you offering me a deal in exchange for some worthless illegible journal?"

"Mrázek, let's put our cards on the table. We know where the donated books Jason was processing came from. It took a lot of effort, but we were able to come up with an inventory and that inventory listed one of the books to be donated as the diary of one James Donelson Walker, who was part of the rebel gang that stole property belonging to the United States. The FBI wants that stolen property back."

"Assuming he did steal something, what makes you say it was property of the United States?"

"Come on, let's not play games. We know and you know—it was a gold shipment confiscated by the United States as war reparations and was being shipped to Memphis to be deposited to the account of the United States of America."

Kole rebutted, "I think the ownership decision might be up to a judge to decide. It seems to me that Mr. Walker was just recovering gold that the Union was trying to steal from the Confederacy."

"As far as you are concerned, the FBI is the judge and the jury. Where is the book?"

Kole decided to continue stringing his captor along. "Let me understand. You snatched me off the street just to tell me that if I get you that smelly old book you will let me go—free and clear. You will forget I am illegal?"

"Free and clear."

"Can you do that—make me legal? Do you have that authority?"

"Cut the shit! You know that I'm not going making you a citizen or something. Just get the book, and I will forget I ever saw you. Things will just go back to how they were before I came along."

Kole's confidence was growing. This guy was coming off more like a thug than a professional law officer. So, Kole decided to confront him. "I get the feeling that you are op-erating outside of your official role. I will offer you a deal. Assuming you are FBI and pursuing this gold on behalf of the United States, I will get the book for you, but I want a green card."

The man sneered, "I'm tired of this garbage." He started to turn away, stopped, and mockingly told Kole exactly what to expect next. "I'm going to turn off the light, lock the door, and let you enjoy the dark while I get dinner and breakfast. When I come back, we will see if you still want to be a funny man."

CHAPTER 24

Mark Rollins

The Gulfstream G-100 rolled to a stop at the Signature flight support facility terminal. Signature is the Fixed Base Operator, FBO, serving General Aviation at the Asheville Regional Airport in Fletcher, North Carolina. Fletcher is about fifteen miles from Asheville's business district. The FBO had a rental car, a silver Lexus, waiting for Rollins and Tony as they landed. It was a short twenty minute drive on Interstate 26 West to the bed and breakfast location. Door to door, the travel time from the Women's Health Club in Brentwood, Tennessee to the Applewood Manor in Asheville was a little over two hours and an hour of that was in the air.

Following the instructions Jennifer McConnell had given Mark, he bypassed the main Applewood Manor house and had Tony drive directly to the facility's detached Cortland Cottage where the fall breakers were staying. Tony usually stays with the car unless he is otherwise needed. This was one of those otherwise days. Rollins wanted Tony with him when he talked to Jason and his companion. His experience has been that an extra pair of ears and another brain always pays dividends especially when interviewing people. The two students had obviously been anxiously awaiting Mark Rollins' arrival because the door flew open before he was able to knock.

"You're Mr. Rollins, aren't you?" asked Jason as he stuck out is hand.

"Yes, I am, and you must be Jason. This is Tony Caruso who is assisting me on this trip."

"God, we are so glad to have you here!" Jason said. Gesturing, he added, "This is my friend, Ella Blakeford."

Ella stepped forward and shook hands with Rollins and Tony. "Boy, do I second that!" Relieved that the cavalry that was going to make things right had arrived, she continued talking without pause. "We really need your help. We reported our friend missing, but the police think we're lying or it's a prank. They won't help us, and we are afraid that something bad has happened to Kole. The three of us are in Asheville working on a project."

Rollins said, "Let's sit down somewhere so you can fill us in." Jason led Rollins and Caruso to the small table with four chairs.

Ella asked, "Can I get either of you anything? We don't have much, but I do have water."

"I would rather we spend our time talking," said Mark as he sat down. "I need the two of you to start from the very beginning. Jason, your mother said that she thinks the three of you are, to quote her, 'up to something.' Are you and what is it? Before you answer, let me explain—you must be absolutely truthful for me to help you."

Jason slouched in one of the chairs as if the air had suddenly gone out of him. Ella's face reddened. There was an uncomfortable pause. Then Jason collected himself and spoke. "I think it is fair to ask that. The only thing important to us right now is finding our friend, Kole."

Ella seemed relieved and eager to explain. "Jason works for the Belmont University library, and he found an unusual volume, an old journal, when he was checking in donated books. It was a diary, and he kept it because he thought the library would not want the old handwritten thing. The book belonged to a Confederate soldier." She paused and almost whispered, "We discovered the diary told where he hid a lot of gold."

"No, no, no! You are summarizing. Leaving out the color." Rollins explained, "I want the details. Go to the very beginning and tell me step by step what happened and with each step what you did."

Ella took a deep breath. Jason took over the conversation, and if he skipped a detail Ella interrupted and added the missing information. After almost three intense hours, Jason said, "And that's when I called my mother, and she called you."

Tony, who along with Mark Rollins, had listened intently asked, "And all you found were some iron cannon balls?"

"Well," said Jason. "We did not actually see them. Our instruments indicated the presence of a lot of iron—we just figured it was iron cannon balls."

Mark said, "Let's go over Kole's disappearance again. Yesterday, after flying the drone, all three of you came back to this cottage. No one left. You took a nap or waited until about seven and then went to Applewood's dining room for breakfast. You came back to the cottage, again all three of you, and went to sleep."

"Yes," replied Ella.

"When you woke up, there were fresh groceries that you believed Kole purchased from some nearby store. It was the same neighborhood store where he had shopped the prior day—the day of your arrival in Asheville, correct?"

"Yes, and we found his note." Jason retrieved the note and gave it to Rollins.

"What about a receipt from the store? Do either of you have that?"

"No, neither Ella nor I saw a receipt of any kind."

"Okay, that is not important right now. But it does bring up the issue of all the other missing breadcrumbs."

"What do you mean?" asked Jason.

"Evidence that Kole exists at all. That he is a real, breathing, walking, talking human being. Make sure I understand. You have no photographs of Kole. He had no phone. You certainly do not have a phone number for him. You have an email address, but it is a Gmail account using some humorous fictitious name that cannot be traced to him. You and Ella registered at this B&B but not Kole. You do not even know, or can't remember, his last name, and even though he seemed to be a Belmont student, he wasn't."

Looking sheepish, Ella and Jason indicated that as hard as that was to believe, it was the truth. Jason said, "I never knew what classes he had. What I do know is that he is very smart and wanted to be an engineer. I can't believe he is not actually enrolled. He came to student events, the student center, and the dining hall. He showed up at the library all the time. And on weekends, he and I would go metal detecting or checking out nearby caves."

Ella added, "To be on campus, he must have had a student ID."

Rollins replied, "He could have used someone else's ID or had a counterfeit ID."

Ella countered, "That doesn't explain why he didn't enroll. Couldn't he have just used his fake ID?"

"I don't think he is using his real name. That would explain it. There would be no way for him to transfer grades from his real name to his fake name. He is probably hanging around the University hoping he can figure a way to qualify for enrollment."

Clearly frustrated, Ella pleaded, "I don't understand what any of this means. Is he a spy or something? Mr. Rollins, does this make any sense to you?"

Jason asked, "What about the witness protection program?"

Mark Rollins shook his head. "If he were in witness protection, he would have enrolled and would have had solid identification. It just would have been manufactured. No, this scenario fits only one answer. He is hiding, running from something or someone. Whoever he is hiding from could be either the good guys or the bad guys. That is just something we are going to have to discover. But that could be the answer as to why he is missing. It could be that whoever he is running from has him, or they have spotted him, and he is on the run again."

Everyone was silent for several minutes—clearly thinking over Mark's speculation. Then Mark broke the silence. "Let me see the diary." Ella got up went to her backpack and brought the book to the table and handed it to Rollins.

As he opened the book and began turning each of the pages that had been taped back into their original places, Rollins looked at his driver and said, "Tony, see if you can get us rooms at this B&B or a nearby hotel. We are going to be spending the night in Asheville."

CHAPTER 25

Applewood Manor

While Tony worked on the accommodations, Mark decided to take a little self-guided tour of the Applewood Manor property. During the flight from Nashville, he had visited the B&B's website to learn a little about the place. It seems that when 44-year-old Captain Perry was disabled in 1903 during his Army service in the Philippines, he retired to Asheville for his health with his wife, Charlotte, and daughter, Anne. While his exact medical condition was not known, he probably suffered some type of lung damage, possibly tuberculosis. He purchased the site for his home on Cumberland Circle in 1908. The site is on the northern edge of what is now the Montford Historic District adjacent to downtown Asheville. The property rises to a knoll that in 1908 overlooked the rolling agricultural lands stretching north along the old Buncombe Turnpike. That view unfortunately has been lost behind growing trees and the continued growth of the city. The grounds, however, are still a relaxing delight, filled with giant wild cherries, apple trees, oaks, pines, and maples, some planted by the original owner. The trees and a variety of flora have turned the grounds into a botanical garden. Captain Perry hired the renowned Asheville architect, William Henry Lord, to design Applewood and its foundation was laid by the same stonemasons who worked on the Biltmore Estate.

As impressive as the exterior and grounds were, Mark still was not prepared for the splendor inside Applewood Manor. It isn't your grandparents' B&B. The luxurious interior echoes Montford's historic character with eclectic-yet-cozy classic and contemporary upscale furnishings. Rollins, an art collector in his own right, was especially struck by the original art collection on display and peppered among the art were framed pieces of history—a portrait of Captain John Adams Perry himself, the original architectural drawings by William H. Lord, and the portrait of Captain Perry's father, U.S. Army Brigadier General Alexander James Perry. One item in particular caught his eye. It was a hand drawn map of Asheville as of 1865. That is the year that Corporal James Walker says he buried the shipment. Mark could not help but think that somewhere in the places shown on that map was a fortune in gold waiting to be discovered.

After checking out the public areas of the Manor, he discovered Applewood's large patio—a beautifully landscaped area floored with native stone and frequently the venue for weddings and other large events. The patio also provided space for small private gatherings or dinners and for guests who just wanted to relax and enjoy the setting and fresh mountain air. Mark found one of those areas to call his own, picked the chair with the best view, and called his team back in Brentwood. Bryan answered on the first ring. "Been waiting for your call Chief, what can the Brain Trust do for you?" Bryan and Mark have worked together for a long time and years ago they gave up the tradition for Southern chit-chat niceties.

"Bryan, we have a missing person, a male. There are no photographs of him, no phone, no address, no history we can find. His age is unknown but likely to be twenty to twenty-five. The missing youth goes by the given name of Kole, surname unknown, and his last known location is the Cortland Cottage at Applewood Manor in Asheville, North Carolina, but he traveled there from Nashville. The last known location while in Nashville was Belmont University. His known associates include Jason Stewart McConnell and Ella Grace Blakeford both Belmont University students and the current occupants of Cortland Cottage. The missing male was known to have made food and drink purchases on two occasions, one today and one yesterday, from what his associates described as a nearby corner grocery store. He also appears to have purchased, or been provided with, unusual and expensive pieces of equipment intended to search for buried gold in the Asheville area. That equipment includes a DJI Phantom 4 drone with a DroneRover sensor attachment and also a Minelab handheld extreme depth metal detector model GPZ 7000.

"Bryan, I want you and your team to find the missing youth if you can, but also fill in the missing pieces—all the unknowns including who the heck is he."

"Wow Chief, you are not asking much. That's a lot of missing pieces to fill in and not much solid information to start with. Next, you'll tell me that you want those missing pieces within the hour."

Rollins looked at his watch. It was already one thirty in the afternoon. "No, I'll give you until five tonight for a progress report and until tomorrow morning for an update."

"Thanks, who needs sleep anyway," sighed Bryan. "We will give it all we've got, starting now." With that said, Bryan disconnected.

Tony found Mark on the patio. "Mr. R, the folks at Applewood have a suite we can share for a couple of days. Has a funny name. They call it the Northern Spy suite."

"Tony, I read a little about the B&B. All their rooms are named after apple varieties."

"Northern Spy is an apple?"

"Yep, and the cottage is named after another apple, the Cortland."

"If you say so, Mr. R. I have already taken our bags up. The Northern Spy is on the fourth floor. They tell me it used to be Captain Perry's sleeping quarters. I checked it out. The suite looks out the front of the house with a view of Town Mountain and the Manor's south lawn. The place has plenty of room. I will bunk in the sitting room, so the bedroom is yours. And the innkeeper, Robin, said the staff would prepare dinner for the four of us—you, me, and the Cortland guests. I took the liberty of letting the students know that we would meet for a working dinner at six tonight. Oh, are you up for a teatime snack? Robin has sent freshly baked cookies to our room plus some other treats and there is a local wine on ice."

Rollins chuckled, "What are we standing around here for! Lead the way, Tony."

CHAPTER 26

Bryan's Report

At five in the evening, Bryan called.

"Chief, I think we have found some of the missing pieces for you. First, his photo and name. That corner grocery store has an impressive security setup. It is much more sophisticated than one would expect, not sure why. We hacked it and picked out your guy rather quickly— a male meeting our description, in his early twenties who purchased bread, cheese, liter bottles of cokes and snack foods, all within our targeted period of two consecutive days. We ran the picture though the U.S. facial identification system and came up empty-handed. So, we know our target is probably not a U.S. citizen or legally in our country. We decided to take our photo and look elsewhere. Chief, do you remember Oliver Bakalar?"

"Sure, he was the member of the Brain Trust who went on sick leave for cancer."

"Well, he is back with us. It was leukemia which is in remission."

"That is great to hear. He is an exceptionally talented member of the team."

"Oliver was from Bohemia, part of what is now the Czech Republic. He remembered that there is village named Koleč. If you translated that to Americanized English, it is Kole. Since our missing person has no U.S. history, Oliver thought maybe he is Czech. So, our man started looking in Czech social media with our facial recognition system and got a hit. Your missing young guy is Kole Mrázek, grandson of František Mrázek, AKA, the Czech Godfather. František, or in English Francis, is now deceased, and a new boss has taken over organized crime in the Republic. What was left of Francis' inner circle and family were *personae non gratae* and hightailed it to the United States. The missing youth, Kole, was apparently separated, maybe estranged, from the family and came across the southern border without checking in with the guards. He is what they call a gotaway."

"Bryan, for the millionth time, you have worked magic."

"Chief, we are not done yet. You asked about the exotic equipment. Top guys in František Mrázek's organization have set up shop in Miami. They run a commercial real estate firm and are considered upstanding businesspeople, at least on the surface. We did not bother to search for underworld activity. The point is they are the source of Kole's funds. We found that the organization has a Nashville law firm on retainer and transfers money and ships packages to the law firm, intended for Kole's use. We know this because we happen to have an inside contact at the law firm, a legal secretary that dates one of our Brain Trust team members. She told our guy that one of the firm's attorneys delivers the packages and cash to a young man. She said the lawyer thinks the guy is in the witness protection system or something like that because he always wants those deliveries made in places where he cannot be seen. It appears to us that whatever Kole asks for Miami delivers. The top guy acts like a real godfather to the boy. His organization provided Kole with both the drone and the handheld extreme depth metal detector. Both purchased through the real estate firm."

"Bryan, that means that Kole's disappearance could be related to his illegal alien status or as a target of his grandfather's enemies."

"That's the way we see it, Chief."

"Well, that gives you something else to work on. The undocumented immigrant issue should be easy—ICE or Homeland Security records should tell us if they are involved. But where do we look if his disappearance is related to the enemy issue?"

"Chief, our guys have some ideas, and we are already working on them. Hopefully, I can tell you something tomorrow, at the morning update."

"Okay, Bryan. I am having a working dinner with Kole's two friends tonight. Maybe, I will come up with something new that will help. I'll be waiting for your call in the morning."

CHAPTER 27

Working Dinner

Rollins opted to have their dinner on the patio rather than in the Manor's large dining room. It was one of those delightful nights when the temperature and humidity are in balance as only happens in the mountains.

The staff had prepared a gigantic paella with accompanying homemade Sangria. Robin stopped by the table to make sure her guests were happy with the service. "Is everything to your liking, Mr. Rollins?"

"Please call me Mark. Yes, everything was wonderful. And let me tell you I have not had anything like your paella outside of Spain—Bomba Spanish rice, several kinds of sausages, shrimp, mussels, clams, peppers, tomatoes, and seasoned to perfection."

"I'm glad you like it, Mark. Thank you for choosing Applewood Manor. I wish it was under better circumstances. We were quite concerned when the police arrived. Ella explained about their friend and today Mr. Caruso, told us that you and he were helping search for the boy. We are praying for him and all of you."

After the Robin left them, they turned back to the work at hand. Rollins was thinking that it would have been a perfect night topped with a perfect meal if not for the seriousness of the situation. The search for Kole would have to wait until Rollins' team back in Tennessee found something to give him an idea of where to start looking. As for the missing gold, Ella had brought out the diary as soon as they finished with dinner and Mark began carefully comparing the original pages to their UV light photographs. Jason explained, "Ella and I have gone over those pages a thousand times looking for something that we might have missed—a clue of some kind. We know the train was robbed. We know that Corporal Walker was part of the gang that took the gold. His description of where the gold was buried is too detailed to just be a fictional story. We either got the directions wrong or there must be some coded message that alters the directions or points to the real location of the gold."

Tony took a sip of the Sangria and as he put down his glass, he countered, "Of course, there is always the possibility that someone has already taken the gold."

Ella conceded, "I feel like we have failed. I don't want to admit it, but that's what I keep thinking. The gold is just gone, or it was never there in the first place."

Rollins snapped, "Really? You think someone dug out the gold from the tunnel that had been blown up, replaced it with cannon balls and blew up the tunnel for a second time? Come on, guys!"

Mark Rollins' challenging voice startled Jason and Ella. He had their undivided attention as he continued. "That scenario does not make any sense. What might make sense is that the Confederate train robbers knew that they were being watched by Asheville's townspeople. The robbers wanted those people to believe something important was being buried in the tunnel. General Welch and his men were aware that the Union troops were close behind and the troops would, of course, question the citizens of Asheville. The train robbers were hoping that their misdirection would provide a good diversion. One that would keep the troops busy while they hid the gold elsewhere and got out of the town without being caught. If that assumption is correct, and I believe it is, our train robbers went through the motions of hiding the gold shipment for show using the cannon balls in place of the actual gold."

Jason perked up. "Yeah, I can see that now."

"However," explained Mark, "My guess is that in the end, it wasn't necessary. The troops apparently did not stay and search for the gold. I'm not sure why yet. Probably they rode past Asheville still chasing what they thought was the wagon carrying the gold."

"But why repeat the false story in the diary?" asked Ella.

"I think Corporal Walker was still hiding the location of the gold, this time from prying eyes," answered Rollins. Then almost as an aside while he continued to read a page in the diary he said, "And I do not think he would have done that without leaving a clue to the real location. We just must be smart enough to find the clue and figure out what it means."

With a downfallen expression, Jason said, "If there is a clue there, I admit I am too blind to see it."

"Mark looked directly at the two young people and assured them, "It's there—we just have to do the hard thing, THINK!"

No one said anything. Tony, Ella, and Jason sat quietly. They were watching Rollins and letting things soak in. They were thinking.

CHAPTER 28

Interrogation

For Kole, it had been a long night. He had only two choices—sleep in the straight back chair or on the hard surface of the cabin's floor. He chose both, switching uncomfortably between the two and trying to stay warm. The man had left him with an old army blanket, but the cold seemed to go right through it. Between being cold and uncomfortable, he got very little sleep. He spent most of the night sizing up the situation. He finally ruled out escaping on his own. There was no way he could break the chain or get to the eye bolt securing the chain. He went over the odds of being rescued. He thought about Jason and Ella. How would they have reacted to his being missing. He was sure they would have gone to the police. Other than that, he couldn't think of any way they could figure out what had happened to him, much less rescue him. Then he thought about his uncle and friends in Miami. They were the most likely to come looking for him, but he put the odds very low of being rescued by his uncle's men—how would they know where to look? He was on his own. He didn't know how but he did know that if he was to get out of this alive, it was going be up to him. As for the FBI man, he was sure that he was operating outside of his FBI role. He was a renegade. Kole thought he had to outsmart him—look for a window of opportunity.

It was morning. He could tell by the light filtering through the material used to cover the room's one window and by the birds. They, too, were awake and singing.

He heard the cabin door open and close. Then the door to his room opened and the FBI man entered and stood picking his teeth. A reminder of the breakfast Kole hadn't had. "Okay kid, I'm back and it's a new day. So, what is it going to be—you ready to play ball?"

Kole demanded, "Where is your partner? I know you FBI guys don't work alone."

"He is off doing other things. Right now, it's just you and me."

"So, the FBI is interrogating me—one FBI agent without any witnesses, with no recording equipment, and no stenographer. This is rubbish and you know it!"

"Okay, funny boy. You can think what you want to about the FBI. But the facts are, I got your ass locked up in this room. Nobody knows where you are. In fact, nobody knows who you are. Maybe you are just a figment of your friends' imagination. So, what you need to consider is that me, myself, and I, can do anything I want to you, and no one is going to know. I can skin you. I can hang you. I can kill you anyway I like if you don't give me that diary."

Kole wanted to keep him talking. "All right, all right—tell me again what happens if I get you the book?"

"I let you go free, and you can go back to whatever it is that you do."

"Maybe you are FBI. If are you are, you've got to be off the ranch, flying solo. You want the gold and you want it for yourself, *úplně sám*, as we say in Czech—all alone."

"Okay kid, I'll just get it myself. But your friends may get hurt. It will be your fault, and you will have to live with that."

"No, I will get you the stinking book! And you are not going touch me or my friends. We have already searched for the gold—where it's supposed to be according to the diary, and it's NOT there. Someone got to it first. You are welcome to dig up the Masonic Lodge parking lot to your heart's content because that's where the diary says it is. But the only thing you are going to find is a bunch of old Civil War cannon balls."

The FBI guy signed wearily. "Yeah, so you say. Look, just give me the book, kid!"

"I will, but I can't promise that you won't be the one to get hurt."

The FBI agent let out an enormous laugh. "I'm shaking in my boots. Just who is going hurt me?"

"My grandfather may be dead but his organization is not, and it moved here—to the states. They have not received my daily call. So, they will have started looking. And they will be looking here soon."

The macho agent seemed to wilt just a little. But he had gone too far to retreat now. And he was too arrogant and sure of himself to be afraid, especially of something he hadn't seen, heard, or even smelled. "So, are going to get the book for me or what?"

"Let me use your phone, and I will call my friends."

"No way. You think I'm an idiot! I see what you're doing. You actually believe you are smart enough to set me up! I tell you what—you just sit and relax. Enjoy what time you have left on this earth. I just might decide to shorten your stay when I come back."

CHAPTER 29

Gangsters and Cheaters

After the working dinner, Rollins studied copies of the diary pages well into the night before finally turning in around midnight. He was awakened early the next morning by a phone call from Bryan.

"Chief, I have a few more answers to fill in those blank spaces. The missing friend is not completely off the grid. He has a phone although it is a burner and an apartment in a mid-town high-rise under the name of Will Frost. By the way, the Czech name Mrázek translates to Frost in U.S. English. l would be happy to tell you how my geniuses found all that out, but you probably don't care about the trivia."

"Not true, Bryan. I am always interested in how you find clues and missing information, but let's save it for another day. Right now, I am more interested in why he tries to stay under the radar. Why use a burner phone? Why rent an apartment under an alias? Who is he afraid of and have they snatched him?"

Bryan said, "We know he is illegal. However, we hacked ICE and Homeland Security servers and found no evidence that they have any interest in Kole Mrázek, Will Frost, or any Czech illegal matching his description."

Rollins, rubbing his forehead, responded to Bryan's report. "If no one is after him for being illegal, then we must conclude that somebody does not like the boy. He is afraid and hiding from someone who is after him. Who is it?"

"Agreed. We are working on it." replied Bryan.

Rollins growled, "It seems to me that nothing is left other than the Czech Republic and Czech organized crime syndicates. That's where we are going to have to start digging. That's all I can think of right now."

"Chief, before we run off to Czech country, you need to know that we came across a strange coincidence that might open another possibility."

"Tell me more, Bryan. You know how I feel about coincidences."

"That's why I'm bringing it up. What appears as a coincidence usually does not happen by accident. And I think before we go deep into Europe, this coincidence just might be what we are looking for."

"Go on."

"Our facial recognition system identified an FBI agent in the same corner grocery store where our missing youth bought his items. It just seemed a little odd to us. So, I assigned one of our guys, Big John Felts, to find out more about that agent and what he might be doing in a small corner grocery store in Asheville, North Carolina."

"And?"

"Chief, I don't know if you are familiar with the dig at Dents Run?"

"Of course, I am. It was a big deal at the time. The FBI brought an army and heavy equipment to Dents Run,

Pennsylvania and began excavating. The people in the small community assumed that they were looking for the legendary Civil War gold that disappeared somewhere in that state's mountains. If I remember the story correctly, in 1863 a caravan of Union soldiers transporting a shipment of gold disappeared in those mountains and all that was ever found of them was their wagons."

"Right, Chief. Now for the kicker—the Washington based agent-in-charge of that dig, Walter Anderson, is the same guy shopping in that neighborhood store. And consider this Chief, the FBI had been in negotiations with treasure hunters who believed they had located the gold. They wanted a finder's fee. The FBI claimed that the dig was a bust. They found no gold. The treasure hunters believe to this day that the gold was there and that the FBI cheated them. Those are the basics. There is more to the story if you want them. We found a detailed article in *The Atlantic,* July/August 2022 issue titled *A Mad Hunt for Civil War Treasure.*"

"Bryan, this must be related to Kole's disappearance. If they cheated treasure hunters once and it paid off for them, why not do it again? Of course, we do not know if the FBI really found the gold, and if they did, did they return it to the United States Treasury or put it in their own pockets? Let's start looking for that FBI agent. What's his name?"

"Agent Walter M. Anderson."

CHAPTER 30

Agent Walter M. Anderson

Agent Anderson is fifty-nine years old and beginning to look it—thinning hair and a pale complexion that testifies to his current paper-pushing position in the Federal Bureau of Investigation. He now carries two hundred forty-nine pounds on his six foot frame with a growing beer belly. He did not always look this way.

At eighteen, with a one hundred and sixty-five pounds of lean muscle honed by the weight room and high school basketball, he became a new Marine recruit heading for Parris Island. By twenty, he was leading a platoon of men breaking down doors to kill terrorists in Afghanistan. At twenty-three, he was back in the states. A rising star with test scores placing his IQ in the very top of the corps, he was enrolled at Wharton on the government's dime, studying economics. At twenty-seven, with his master's degree, he was back on active duty, a major in the intelligence wing stationed at Quantico, Virginia. At thirty, he left the Marines for the FBI.

He was hired as a special agent. It was an opportunity he could not turn down, a chance to become part of the most prestigious law enforcement agency in the U.S. charged with the job of National Security. He would be fighting organized crime, public corruption, terrorism, violent crime, and attacks involving weapons of mass destruction.

What he had not expected were the memos-to-file and the reports. Endless pieces of paper to be written or read and filed. As the years passed, the glimmer on his pure gold FBI badge didn't seem as bright. Then one day, he had two visitors, Glen and Daniel Mallet. They were treasure hunters who told him about buried Civil War gold. The gold they said was from the Pennsylvania mint, property of the United States Treasury, and they would show the FBI where it was located for a finder's fee.

Anderson took the story and finder's fee proposal to FBI management. At first, they scoffed at the idea. But after a couple of nights, several beers, and a couple of martinis, they decided to have some of their research people investigate the story of lost gold. The research seemed to substantiate the story. As the FBI's top brass thought about it and talked about it, they began to consider what they could do with the gold if it really existed, and they found it. There were ways to launder what they found, and it could be used as a slush fund. There were always operations that Congress and the Attorney General did not need to know about. And, while no one voiced it aloud, every one of them was thinking that they might dip into the slush fund from time to time for personal needs. After all, government pay was hardly what they were worth. Management began to formulate a plan, a plan that had to include Agent Anderson because he was already involved.

Walter Anderson organized the excavation, brought in the equipment and manpower, dug up the gold and lied to the treasure hunters. The gold left Dents Run in four armored trucks. Except for his one hundred thousand dollar reward, as his management people called it, Anderson never saw another dime of the gold. Nor did any of the gold ever make it to the United States Treasury.

After years as an agent, he had learned that intimidation was an effective tool, and he began to take on a tough guy, bad cop, persona when questioning or interviewing people. That behavior labeled him a bully. Now that was topped off by his getting old and being generally pissed off!

He had stumbled onto the college kids and what they were up to. The first clues were the internet searches and especially when those searches involved newspaper articles more than a hundred and fifty years old. A check of Ella's known associates yielded more clues. He identified Kole which led to his connection with the Miami company that just happened to have purchased sophisticated equipment used by treasurer hunters. The final clue was her involvement with Jason McConnell. That lead to the diary. Another agent might have missed the clues or had been too lazy to keep digging but not Anderson. He had been at Dents Run. He had seen gold and handled it. Some people call it gold fever; he had an insatiable appetite for the precious metal. He believed he could smell gold—even taste it. All he needed was to get his hands on the diary. This time when he dug it up, the treasure was going to be all his!

He trumped up an FBI reason to be in Asheville, and as required when pursuing a fugitive, he took along a partner, Kevin Waters, a recent addition to the agency. Waters knew nothing about the students, the diary, or the gold. Nor was he aware of what Anderson was planning or how far he was willing to go to get what wanted. Told that the tip that had brought them to Asheville turned out not to be credible, Waters flew back to D.C. but not before Anderson had him pick up a Royal Enfield INT650 from Asheville Motorcycle Rentals and ride it to the mountain cabin Anderson had rented as their Asheville base of operation.

CHAPTER 31

Ancestry

It was too early for Applewood's breakfast service, but the staff was happy to deliver Mark's requested cup of coffee. What hadn't been requested, but arrived with the coffee, were two toasted slices of homemade bread along with butter from an Asheville creamery together with apple cinnamon jam from a nearby apple orchard. What he had planned to be a five minute stop for coffee turned into a thirty minute, savor every bite, repast. Reluctantly, he had declined the offered third cup of coffee and headed to the cottage.

The weather had turned cooler overnight, and Mark had switched from his usual short sleeved polo to a long sleeved shirt and a quilted vest. The morning was a stark contrast to yesterday's colorful sunset. The overcast sky and light fog gave the mountains their characteristic smokiness. Steam was rising from the French Broad River that runs past the city. The ghostly effect seemed appropriate for the Halloween season. The sun was not yet high enough to light the mountains. That would come later when the rising sun turned the dark moody mountains into a celebration of fall.

When Rollins reached the cottage, Ella ushered him in after answering his knock at the door.

As Rollins said, "Good morning," he noticed the aroma of coffee and saw used cups and plates still on the table. "I can see the two of you have been up a while. I hope you got a decent night's sleep."

"Thanks for asking. I couldn't stop thinking about Kole. That kept me up late and I woke up worrying about him. I don't think Jason fared any better. But we are okay."

"Where is Jason?"

"He's in the shower. Can I get you anything Mr. Rollins?"

Moving to the cottage's small table, Mark replied, "If you have a bottled water, I'll take one."

"We sure do," she replied. "The inn keeps us well stocked." As she opened the door to the small retro style refrigerator, she asked, "Where is Mr. Caruso? Can I get water for him, too?"

"Thanks for the offer, but I sent Tony back to Nashville. He is going to pick up my car and bring it here."

Ella finished removing the used dishes and had just sat down at the table when Jason, showered and dressed for the day, pulled out a chair and joined them. "Oh," he said, "I thought you rented a car."

"I did, but my Lexus has a few special features and communication capabilities that I need in order to stay in touch with my business activities."

Rollins had studied the photographed pages for hours last night, but this morning he wanted to take one more look at the book itself. It was on the table. Ella placed the water bottle next to Rollins who had the diary in his hands and was turning it over and over from front to back. He looked at the couple now seated side by side. "I have studied every damn page so many times that I think I have this book memorized. If there is a hidden message or a clue, it must be on the pages describing the burial of the gold in the abandoned tunnel. Let me change that. Forget what I said. There is no maybe about it! The clue is there. My gut tells me it must be there. I will say it again, we just must be smart enough to find it."

Jason said, "I agree about missing something. Ella and I have been trying to find it. She and I created a game last night. It was to see which of us could find a sentence or paragraph that was not essential. You know, something you can take out that would not change the narrative."

"That is clever, guys. What did you find?"

"It's this. "Jason pointed to the first paragraph of the page giving directions to the gold. Jason continued, "Without damage to the narrative, you can remove these two sentences":

> *I fear the end is near and with the growing belief that our Dixieland is losing to the Union it is best I that write about the shipment in hopes this book of mine will make it to my mother and through her to my sister, Gemma, whose strength of character has been the backbone of our family. If I should die in this Godforsaken place, I do so with the knowledge that Gemma shall care for my mother.*

"But for the life of me, if there is a message in those two sentences, I can't find it!"

Ella said, "My mother has an Ancestry account. I called her and she gave me her login information. I looked for James Donelson Walker and his mother, Margaret Donelson

Walker. There was no family tree for either of them. But I did find them both in other family trees. And if it means anything, I did not find any indication that Mrs. Walker had a daughter. She was a teacher, taught English and Latin. Also, there was nothing about a sister on the family trees where I found James Walker listed. Then I searched for the name Gemma. I found a lot of them but none with the maiden name of Walker."

Rollins read the sentences again and pondered the Ella's ancestry.com search results. Then he turned to Ella and ordered, "Get your laptop."

She felt a surge of excitement. Had Rollins thought of something? Returning with the laptop, she sat down putting the computer on the table opened and ready for use. "Now what, Mr. Rollins?"

"Go to Google and search for 'Gemma Name.' Tell me what you find."

Ella typed the search request and pressed the enter key. A second later, Google responded with the answer. Ella exclaimed, "Wow!" She looked at Jason smiling. Then she turned to Rollins. "Google says, Gemma is a girl's name of Latin origin, meaning gem or jewel."

Rollins smiled back. "What is the other unusual word in those sentences?"

Ella and Jason both looked at the photographed page and the sentences thinking hard to conjure up the key word.

Jason shouted as he jumped up knocking over his chair. "Backbone, Backbone! How freaking stupid of me? All my life I have done two things to any old book I managed to get my hands on. Ella, quick—do you have a pair of tweezers?"

She answered without hesitation. "YES, yes of course!" She crossed the room, grabbed her overnight bag, and began digging through its contents. "Got them," she shouted, running to hand the tweezers to Jason.

Holding the tweezers up like a trophy Jason declared, "The two things I always did was first to look between the pages and second to search for anything hidden in the book's spine—its backbone. "He inserted the tweezers carefully and gently pulled out the answer that they had been searching for.

CHAPTER 32

FBI Comes Calling

The spine had given up a thin strip of fragile paper on which was written in script the words:

Gold is buried in an abandoned battlement dug at the end of Academy Street near Glenn's Creek.

When the excitement had settled down, Rollins tried to caution the two students. "Don't get your hopes too high. You still must find the gold. The message, like the text on the page, might not be real or even if it is, the gold may have been found years ago."

Jason's iPhone began playing the laughing scene from The *Treasure of The Sierra Madre*. A little embarrassed, he put the phone on the speaker and said, "Hello."

"This is Robin," she whispered. "There is a man here who says he is from the FBI. He came to the main house asking for you, and I told him you were staying in the cottage. He is on his way over there now."

"Maybe it is about our missing friend. I'll let you know later. Thanks for telling me."

As Jason disconnected the call, Rollins said, "I am going to duck out of sight. I have reason to believe this guy is not on the up and up. It's best that he thinks you and Ella are alone—that no one else is here to overhear if he gets out of line, which I expect." Over his shoulder as he began moving, he shouted, "And don't let him intimidate you!"

Ella and Jason both nodded.

There was a knock at the door. Jason hesitated, thinking of what to say in view of Rollins' warning. The knocking changed to pounding and a loud voice shouted, "FBI. OPEN THE DOOR!"

Jason quickly rushed to the door and opened it. But he stood in the doorway, blocking the entrance.

The man wore aviator sunglasses and smiled as he said, "I assume you are Jason Stewart McConnell, are you not?" The smile didn't really seem friendly. It seemed artificial and threatening.

"Let's go inside," commanded the man.

"Wait a minute. I want to see your credentials," snapped Jason.

The man, Agent Walter Anderson, pulled out a leather identification wallet. He flipped it open for Jason to see and just as quickly flipped it closed.

"Just a minute. You didn't give me time to study the badge or your ID card. You didn't give me time to compare you to the picture on the ID card either."

"Look, Mr. McConnell, I showed you my ID. Now, step aside and let me in."

"Do you have a warrant?"

The agent's short laugh was dismissive. "You've been watching too many cop shows on TV. I don't need a warrant. Now get out of the way. I have some questions and I want some answers."

"Why? What are you investigating?"

"Shit," the agent muttered as he started to muscle his way into the cottage, but at that moment, Ella joined Jason in the doorway. Side by side, they filled the doorframe. Her arrival made the agent step back.

"What is your name, Agent?" Ella barked in an unusually authoritative voice for her.

Ignoring her, the man continued, "What the hell, McConnell? You got to bring in your girlfriend as reinforcements?"

Ella spoke up, "The name is Ella Grace Blakeford to you. Now I'll ask you again, what is yours?"

"Okay, Miss Blakeford. It's Agent Walter M. Anderson. Now, can the three of us go inside for a nice little chat?"

Jason responded, "Agent Anderson, I am asking you again. What do you want to talk to us about?"

Anderson was gritting his teeth as he hissed, "Both of you are asking for trouble!" He took a deep breath. "Actually, you have just about crossed the line! Obstruction of justice is a felony, and I will haul your butts out of here in handcuffs if you don't let me in right now!"

Jason and Ella did not make any move and continued to guard the doorway. Bravely, her voice raised, Ella challenged. "We asked you what you are investigating?" After a pause, she added as if an afterthought—"And, I would like the name and phone number of the Assistant United States Attorney who is in charge of whatever case you are working on."

Before the agent could respond to Ella, Jason added, "And, you are not coming into this room without a warrant."

Anderson was frustrated and surprised that his bullying had not worked against these two kids. However, he was savvy enough from his years of dealing with suspects or witnesses to know he had to change tactics.

"Okay, let's start over." Then speaking slowly and politely, he said, "I understand you are standing up for your rights. Here is my badge and ID, take your time to study them."

Jason knew what to look for. He had read it on the internet just messing around. The badge was clearly solid gold. The words 'Federal Bureau of Investigation' at the top and 'Department of Justice' at the bottom were fully spelled out. He had read that fakes often use abbreviations. The picture on the ID card matched the man standing in front of him. Jason looked at Ella and shrugged, turned to the agent, and returned the badge wallet.

"Now, you two are not suspects in any investigation. However, we are investigating an associate of yours, Kole Mrázek."

Taken aback, Ella's hands went to her heart as she uttered, "Oh God!" It was the first time she had heard the name Mrázek, but she knew it was their Kole. Recovered, she said to the agent, "We have been looking for him!" Then pleading, she added, "Do you know where he is?"

"Not at this time," lied Anderson.

Jason, still on guard, his voice raised said, "Investigating him for what?"

"Mr. Mrázek is an illegal alien with ties to a known Czech criminal organization based in Florida."

"That's absurd," exclaimed Ella.

Jason backed her up. "Look, Agent Anderson, we find your accusation about Kole unbelievable. Even if it is true, we are still not prepared to let you in without a warrant. Now, if you want us to go to the nearest FBI office, we will be happy to comply. Of course, our attorney will accompany us."

"Bullshit, I don't have time for you two and your lawyer crap. You have just added yourself to our suspect list. We will be in touch." With that the agent turned on his heels and headed back to his car. Out of hearing range, he mumbled to himself, "You assholes have not seen the last of me. I am having that book one way or another—no matter what it takes."

While the back and forth was going on at the front door, Rollins sent a text message to Robin at the Manor's main house. "PLS-get make, color, license # of alleged agent ASAP. Explain later."

CHAPTER 33

The Agent's Car

"I got it, Mark. It was a dark gray Toyota Camry rental. I know it is a rental because it has a barcode on the windshield and passenger side window. That's a giveaway!"

"What about the license number, Robin?"

"Somebody installed one of those covers that intentionally makes it difficult, almost impossible, to read the plate. I could see some of it, but not all of it at once. Different pieces of the plate are readable depending on the angle of view. I could tell it was a North Carolina OBX plate ending in the letter A, and I got the first number, two, and last two numbers, four and three. Then I saw the agent coming from the cottage and I ran back in the house before I could get the missing number."

"That's okay, Robin. You did great, what you have given me will really help."

"Mark, there is one more thing. We have a *plein air* class scheduled for today. The easels had already been set up. I borrowed a brush and a little Titanium White. Now his car has a white 'X' on its roof. It's not very big but find the X and you'll have the right car!"

"Very clever! You are one smart lady."

"Is everything all right? Do I need to be concerned about my guests in the Cortland Cottage?"

"There is nothing for you to worry about. They are straight up kids. As I mentioned earlier, I'm here to help them find their missing friend. I will bring you up to date after I find out more about the would be FBI Agent that showed up at your door."

"Okay, thanks Mark."

There was someone else at the door of the cottage. Jason hesitated, then turned to Ella. "Will you see who it is? I cannot deal with another FBI visitor."

After his conversation with Robin, Mark returned to the cottage joining Tony on the steps just as his second round of knocking ended. "Tony, you are back just in time." Ella opened the door. Rollins turned his attention to her. "Ella, Tony and I are going to leave you and Jason while we track down a couple of things."

Ella still shaken by the FBI man and about Kole asked, "What should Jason and I be doing while you are gone?"

"Sit tight and try to relax until we get back. I am going to find out more about your FBI caller and all that business about Kole." With that said, Rollins put a hand on Tony's shoulder and said, "Glad you're back. Take me for a drive."

CHAPTER 34

Mycroft

From the driver's seat, Tony turned to his backseat passenger and asked, "Where to Mr. R?"

"For now, just drive. I have some calls to make."

The voice on the other end of the call answered. "What's up, Chief?"

"Bryan. I need you to track a car currently on the move in or around Asheville including the Blue Ridge Parkway. The car is a Toyota Camry, dark gray with a white X on the roof. Our friendly innkeeper added that touch when I asked her to get the car's ID information. I have a partial for the license plate. I am missing the second digit of its four numbers. It's a North Carolina plate. The first part is OBXC2, the next number is missing, then 43A. You got it?"

"Got it, Chief."

"Okay, I need you to get right on it, like now!"

"Roger," was all Bryan replied before ending the call and moving to one of the computer consoles in his large working office. From that station, he connected the Brain Trust computer with Asheville's traffic camera systems. He moved to a second console and entered the commands that connected him to the cameras on I-26, I-240, I-75 and the Blue Ridge Parkway. Within minutes, Bryan had connected all area traffic cameras to the supercomputer located in a secure section of the Women's Health Club. It was a duplicate of the Frontier system installed at the Department of Energy's Oak Ridge National Laboratory that is considered the fastest computer in the world—and supposedly the only one of its kind. The Brain Trust AI programs began comparing car type, roof, color, and license to the profile target—make, color, license number, and—a white X.

Next, Rollins called Jason. "Jason, get your drone ready. I may need to send it on a mission—ASAP. Stand by for another call. Be ready with the drone."

Jason did not bother to ask why. He just replied, "Will do!"

The third call was to a part time member of the Brain Trust, a man with extraordinary access to highest levels of our government and military. Taking a note from Arthur Conan Doyle, Rollins gave him the code name Mycroft. As Mycroft, his actual name and position within the government or military are unknown to all except Mark Rollins.

"Mycroft, I need a favor. I need the inside scoop or scuttlebutt on an FBI Agent, Walter M. Anderson, and I want to know why he is in Asheville."

"How soon do you need it?"

"I need it now. But I will settle for tonight."

"I'll get back within an hour or two." The call ended.

"Mr. R, I think we have a tail."

"What is it, Tony?"

"Black SUV about two cars back."

"You think it's government?"

"No, it looks like a Land Rover. The government is strictly Chevy—mostly Tahoes and Suburbans."

"Well, let's find out what they want. Pull in at the next overlook that we come to."

"But Mr. R, what if they don't like us?"

"In bright daylight with all the Blue Ridge traffic and sightseers, I don't think they are going to come at us guns blazing. Maybe they just want to talk. But we might as well find out from the comfort of a bullet proof car. You just keep the motor running."

"Makes sense Mr. R, but I am going to keep my baton by my side just in case. The GPS screen listed the next pullover at about twenty miles ahead."

Mark Rollins' mobile phone number is intercepted by special equipment located in Brentwood and is passed on as a normal cell phone signal. However, a duplicate signal is redirected to a satellite system assuring that Rollins is accessible regardless of location, worldwide. The Lexus LS 460 is a mobile communications center giving Rollins full access to the World Wide Web, including the so called cloud— public, dark, and secret. A call came in through the car's communication console. It was Mycroft.

"I believe I have what you need. Anderson was a top notch agent in his younger years. The insiders say he has risen to his level of incompetence and has turned sour on the government and the FBI. My source described him as arrogant, a bully, and one mean son of a bitch. Most agents never fire their gun at anyone. He put five notches on his weapon, just in the last three years. If you ask me, he is a dangerous man—one you should stay away from. He was the in-charge agent for the Dents Run incident that was recently in the news. It was Civil War gold that two treasure hunters thought they had found. The two went to the FBI with what they had found and proposed a finder's fee. The FBI dug for it. Dig was a bust—no gold. At least that is what Anderson told the treasure hunters. Now, here is the part you did not hear from me or anyone else. Understand?"

"Yes, of course."

Mycroft continued. "The Inspector General's Office has opened a Dents Run case file. They have taken the cheated claim of the treasure hunters seriously. There appears to be evidence that the FBI did find gold. They took possession depositing their find to secret accounts—slush funds that could be used to finance projects they do not want Congress to know about. If the Inspector's suspicions are correct, you would expect gold fever to corrupt those involved. That appears to be happening. There are three people in the Agency's leadership who are suspected of being involved. All three have experienced a recent improvement in their quality of life—indications suggest they are sampling funds from the secret accounts for their personal use."

CHAPTER 35

Miami

After Mycroft's call ended, the car's console indicated an incoming call from Bryan Gray. Rollins answered. "Bryan, what have you got for me?"

"We finally spotted the agent's car driving toward the town of Bat Cave, but right now he is on a narrow, winding mountain road without cameras. We'll keep watching for him. When he shows up again on camera, I'll let you know. Chief, there are zillions of remote cabins in the area around that place. If he is staying in one of those, I will not be able to tell you which one without air assets."

Tony interrupted, "Mr. R, the overlook is around this curve."

"Bryan, hold that thought. I will get back with you." Rollins disconnected the call just as Tony drove into the overlook parking area.

Mark had been too busy on the phone to pay attention to the majestic views right outside his car's window. As they pulled into the overlook for Mount Mitchell, he gasped, "Wow, look at that! This must be the peak of their fall color season. You know, Sarah would love this—she would say it's God's palette—blue and white for the sky, then all the golden colors of fall."

"Mr. R, you should take a picture for her. She really has a way with words. I think I will remember that—God's palette."

The black Land Rover had slowed, and for a moment, it seemed like the car would continue to drive past them, but the driver braked hard and turned into the overlook. The SUV stopped on the passenger side of the Lexus leaving about four feet between the cars. Rollins shifted his attention from the view of Mount Mitchell to the Land Rover just as the driver and passenger got out. They walked over to Rollins' vehicle. Both were dressed in black pants, black shirts, and royal blue sportscoats with a panther embroidered on the pocket—not the usual 'Men in Black' attire you would expect if they were from the government. The attire was more appropriate for Florida than the mountains in October. But Rollins knew what the bulge in the otherwise perfectly tailored jackets meant. The older of the two, face well-tanned but pockmarked, knocked on the passenger window. Rollins lowered it a couple of inches.

The older man said, "Yo, you Mark Rollins?" His flattop and accent suggested eastern European.

"Yes, I'm Rollins. What can I do for you two?"

"Mr. Greco from New Jersey said you were a standup guy. My name is Ivan, and this is my associate, Boris. A friend has gone missing. The last time we heard from him, he was on his way to this part of the country. Mr. Greco told our boss that you just took a private jet to Asheville. He said that, knowing you, your flight was too much of a coincidence not to believe that you were looking for our boy that has disappeared. After following you around, we think Mr. Greco was right. You are looking for Kole Mrázek, too. We would like you to tell us what you know about our friend."

"Are you from Miami?"

"Yeah, we are."

Rollins handed Ivan his card with his phone and email address. "Give me your contact information so we can be in touch."

Ivan pulled out his billfold and passed his business card to Rollins. The name on the card was Panther Real Estate. "The name and phone number of my boss is on the back."

"Ivan, I will fill you in on the details later, but what I can tell you is that Kole may be somewhere in the area around the town of Bat Cave. We believe that perhaps he is being held by an FBI agent, Walter Anderson. I suspect that Anderson is a rogue agent and that his retention of Kole is not legit. But I could be wrong." Rollins wrote down the information about the car and passed it to Ivan. "The agent is driving this car. Look for it around Bat Cave. If you find it, call me before taking any action. The man is armed as you are. Let's work together to get Kole out safely."

"Okay, Mr. Rollins. You gotta deal."

"Tony, take me back to Applewood Manor."

As they drove away, Mark said to no one in particular, "Signore Roberto Greco."

Tony gave a chuckle. "That old man has your number."

"Tony, I don't know how he does it? Since I helped him with that situation in 2004 involving his son, the old Don feels that he owes me a debt. No matter where I am traveling, he knows about it. When I step off a plane, he usually has a car and a driver waiting for me. He has a pipeline into the travel and hospitality industry. These days, the old New

Jersey boss has gone mostly legal, but his businesses are still a little gray—cash operations like limo services, gambling, escort services, et cetera. Still, it's uncomfortable for me."

"Right, Mr. R, but it's like you have said—it's never a good idea to decline a Don's offer of help. That could be considered an insult. And it's not healthy to insult a Mafia boss," warned Tony.

"No, it is not, Tony."

CHAPTER 36

Finder's Fee

"Tony, when we get back to Applewood Manor, I want to pick up Jason and the drone then head straight for Bat Cave."

"Sure thing, Mr. R, from where we are now, we have about an hour return drive to Applewood Manor."

Rollins made a quick call to Jason. Ella answered. "Hi Ella, I was calling Jason."

"Oh, hello Mr. Rollins. He's outside in the field testing the drone."

"Let Jason know that I'm on my way to pick him up. I am hoping the drone can locate the agent's car and possibly Kole."

"I will, but I really want to come too. I need to be helping—doing something other than just sitting in this cottage."

"Sure, Ella. But if we do find that car and discover that Anderson has Kole, things might get dicey. Tony and I are trained and have the equipment to take care of ourselves. I don't want you or Jason to get hurt. So, promise me that you will do exactly as you are told to do. If that is to stay in my car, then you stay in the car, agreed?"

"I understand," she said and added, "I promise."

"Okay, find Jason and fill him in. We should be arriving at your place in twenty to thirty minutes—be ready."

Rollins decided to give Mycroft one more mission. Mycroft answered Rollins' call on the second ring and smiling to himself, he answered, "I was expecting you to call again."

"Why is that?"

"That's the way it always is with you, my friend. You always have one more thing you want me to do."

Rollins chuckled. "Well, here is the one more thing. How tight are you with the Secretary of the Treasury?"

"She takes my calls. What do you need from her?"

Rollins explained the details of the gold robbery and the connection of the gold to the fall of Atlanta at the end of the Civil War. "If the three students recover it, is the government likely to claim ownership of the gold? What do you think, Mycroft?"

"No question about it," replied Mycroft. "They will! You remember I talked about the Dents Run gold. Same thing here. Your gold was confiscated as war reparations, and it remains federal property no matter how long ago the robbery occurred."

"That's what I was afraid of," replied Mark. "So, I want you to negotiate a finder's fee, actually three finder's fees. One for each of the young people. I figure the gold is worth around thirty-six million. I want a ten percent finder's fee for each of them—tax free. The Treasury will get seventy percent or twenty-five million and some change. Without the efforts and research of these three treasurer hunters, the government would get nothing."

Mycroft said, "I take it you are thinking that the Secretary can do this under the Kleptocracy Asset Recovery Rewards Program just enacted by Congress?"

"Yes, it gives her that authority."

"Doesn't the bill limit her per deal authority to five million dollars?" asked Mycroft.

"Well, each finder's fee would only be three million six hundred thousand—that is less than the five million limit."

"You don't think they will look past the pieces and consider our request as a ten million plus deal?"

"I know you, Mycroft. You can talk them into rationalizing anything, but the bill also allows her to go above the limit with Presidential approval. Doesn't he also take your calls? You don't have to answer that, I know the answer."

"Okay, Mark let me work the phones and see what I can do. I do not think they want another Dents Run on their hands. So that works in our favor."

"Wait, there is one more thing!"

"Why am I not surprised. Isn't there always one more thing?"

"It is a green card for one of the three—Kole. He is currently a Czech citizen and undocumented. This one more thing is non-negotiable. The kid will enroll in Belmont University."

CHAPTER 37

Bat Cave

As they approached Applewood Manor a little past one in the afternoon, Rollins instructed Tony to stop at the main house first. "Let's make a quick pit stop and see if the staff can make some to go sandwiches. You know, no matter what they throw together for us, it will be better than anything we could get on the road."

"Roger that, Mr. R."

"*Jambon* and *fromage*—ham and cheese on French bread spread with local butter—what more can a person ask for!" Rollins exclaimed as he and Tony thanked the staff and took the basket they had packed for them.

Jason and Ella were outside waiting for them with the drone when Tony drove the car the short distance from the front of the main building to the adjacent cottage. Until now, Rollins had not had a reason to examine the drone. He stepped out of the car to look it over. The four helicopter designed props eliminated the need for a wide wingspan making the drone easy to transport. It fit in the trunk with room to spare.

155

As Mark looked on, Tony was helping Jason load the drone and its control equipment. Seeing the advantage of the helicopter design in action, Rollins remarked, "There is no way the drones Bryan and his team have been flying would have gone in that trunk. We need to add a few of these to our equipment inventory."

The loading complete, Rollins ordered, "Let's hit the road! As the saying goes, we are burning daylight!" Rollins got in the front passenger seat leaving the two students to get in the back of the Lexus where Tony had stashed the basket of food.

As Tony pulled out of the drive, Ella asked, "So, where are we headed?"

"We are going to the small town of Bat Cave. That's where we believe we will find the FBI agent and hopefully Kole. But I need to make sure the agent is still there and that he does not leave while we are in route—so I need to make a call."

Bryan answered with his usual greeting, "Hi Chief, what do you need?"

"What is the status of the agent's car—still in the Bat Cave area?"

"Looks that way. Just to fill you in, Bat Cave, a one street town, is an unincorporated community. It is in Henderson County, but it is still considered part of the Asheville Metropolitan Area. It gets the name from an actual bat cave located on Bluerock Mountain because it's supposed to be home to a heck of lot of bats. And the darn thing is the largest known augen gneiss granite fissure cave in North America! What is important to us, however, is the town's ingress and egress. It is located along the banks of the Broad River, and it is where three highways merge—U.S. Route 64 from Hendersonville, U.S. Route 74A from Asheville, and

TREASURE OF THE DIARY

North Carolina Highway 9 from Black Mountain. While these highways are almost devoid of cameras, the town has two cameras on each of the only three highways in or out of town. They point in opposite directions, one at each end of the town, filming cars coming and going. We observed the agent drive into the town on 74A, and that's it. He must have turned off, on to a local road, going up into the mountains. If he leaves, we will know it."

"Sounds like you have it covered. Let me know the minute things change. I have Jason and Ella with me. We are on our way there with the drone to do some hunting."

"Fantastic. Can I link to the bird?"

"I have no idea, but right now I don't think that's necessary." Rollins ended the call, after reminding Bryan to remain watchful.

Ella asked, "Is there food in the basket?"

"Right," declared Mark. "That's our lunch. Ella, do the honors and pass our treats around."

"Great, I'm starving," she said.

Mark took a couple of bites of the ham and cheese sandwich. It was the French version, one that you can pick up readymade at just about any roadside market in the south of France. He could never understand why the food from our markets could be so bad and the French so good. As he finished his *jambon* and *fromage*, he told Jason and Ella about Ivan and Boris.

"From what I have been able to piece together, Kole is the grandson of a mafia boss back in the Czech Republic. There was war between the two largest Czech crime syndicates, and Kole's family was on the losing end. The grandfather was assassinated, and his successor began hunting down, and eliminating, members of the grandfather's family and inner circle. As many as could fled to the United States. They did it legally. Once here, they went into the real estate investment business. Apparently, they are no longer engaged in criminal activities. They became respectable businesspeople, at least on the surface. Kole was never involved in the family business and was not living in the Czech Republic at the time all this was taking place. But he was still at risk, and like the others, he headed for the United States. However, for some reason, he didn't go through the legalization process. Maybe he panicked or he just didn't think he had time. Nevertheless, he was smuggled across the southern border—what the ICE people call a gotaway. Kole's uncle, head of the Miami enterprise, looks out for Kole, providing him money and anything else he needs. The uncle insists that Kole check in by phone on a regular schedule—every other day."

Ella interrupted, "But Kole doesn't even have a phone."

"Not completely true, Ella. He has what is called a burner—a prepaid cellphone that can't be traced to the user. However, he only used it for the call to Miami."

Jason looked stunned. "All of this blows my mind. What could possibly be next?"

Rollins cleared his throat. "What's next is that when we get to Bat Cave, we will be joined by two men sent here from Miami—Ivan, and Boris. They were dispatched here by the uncle because Kole didn't make his regular check-in call. We agreed to work together to locate Kole and, if needed, to rescue him."

For the next ten minutes, Kole's two friends sat in silence taking it all in. To them Kole had just been one of the amigos—their friend and fellow student. Mark Rollins had pulled back the curtain on Kole's past but in doing so, he revealed Kole as an even greater mystery in their minds. How can he ever be the same person again? He couldn't. He knew things and had experienced things that they never would. Nevertheless, he was still their friend and they desperately wanted to bring him home.

They were nearing Bat Cave, and Rollins decided to break the bad and good news to Jason and Ella. "Guys, I did some checking, and I am sorry to tell you that the buried gold is without question the property of the United States of America. When we dig it up, we should have a United States Treasury Department representative present. Otherwise, it will get messy. If we fail to notify them, they most assuredly will come after the gold."

With resignation, Jason said, "Well, I can't say that we are not disappointed. But Ella and I have been talking, and as much as we wanted it to be finders keepers, the evidence was piling up. Contrary to our initial thoughts, everything we were reading pointed toward government ownership."

"The good news is that my team is negotiating to get you a finder's fee. I cannot guarantee that we will be successful or if successful what the fee will be."

Ella leaned forward and put her hand on Rollins' shoulder. "We can't say enough times how thankful we are that you are helping us."

Jason added, "But what is really important to both of us right now is that we find Kole and that he is okay."

CHAPTER 38

The Rescue

"Ivan, this is Mark Rollins. Have you had any luck finding the agent's car?"

"None. We checked at least a dozen cabins with no luck. There are many cabins around here and none are easy to get to."

"We are on our way to Bat Cave with a drone. My driver tells me we are almost there—five or six minutes. Where can we meet?"

"We saw a place while checking out the town. The Old Cider Mill. You can't miss it. It's on the right just as you enter the town on 74A."

"Got it. Ivan, see if you can spot some open ground nearby for us to set up the drone."

"I know just the spot. It's on your right, about a hundred yards further down the highway from the Cider Mill. The ground around here is hard enough to drive on if you want to meet there."

"Sounds good."

Tony spotted the Cider Mill. He slowed the car looking for the field. The sun was low in the sky and blindingly bright, making it difficult to see anything on Tony's right. The Land Rover flashed its lights and Tony turned off the road pulling up next to Ivan's vehicle. As soon as he stopped, he popped open the trunk. Jason and Ella jumped out of the car to retrieve the drone and its control equipment.

Ivan and Boris walked over from their SUV to join Tony and Rollins as they watched the two students. Jason and Ella worked silently, clearly a little intimidated by the two tough looking Miami men, especially the big one. Ella got down on the ground with the drone's control box. She flinched when Ivan's deep voice interrupted her work. "Look, I can open back of Land Rover. Use cargo floor as table. It will make things easier than working in grass."

A little surprised, she managed a smile and said, "Thank you, that wasn't going to be very comfortable."

Mark Rollins studied a topographic map that Boris had purchased from one of the town's shops catering to hikers. Boris was the younger of the two men from Miami. Where Ivan's clothes were a traditional man's cut, Boris' pants and coat were tailored for a slim fit and unlike Ivan's flattop, Boris' hairstyle was modern—a mid fade to a faux mohawk. With his brooding expression and shirt opened three buttons, he could have stepped right out of *GQ*. However, from the way he handled himself, Rollins knew he was no pretty boy. The man had been around and he knew his stuff. The map was a smart move. Rollins walked over to Jason. Pointing to the map he asked, "Can you program the drone to search these GPS coordinates?"

"Absolutely—consider it done." Within minutes the drone was in the air, flying a search grid pattern over the defined area. With no specific programmable target, all Jason and Ella could do was watch the control unit's video screen in hopes that they would spot the car with its white X on the roof. Tony, Rollins, Ivan, and Boris crowded behind the two students, intently watching over their shoulders. Each time the drone flew over a cabin, Jason paused the search pattern and had the drone circle the cabin looking for any parked automobiles.

Bingo! Forty-five minutes into the search, they spotted the vehicle. The Miami guys copied the GPS coordinates, removed the control unit, and started to take off in the Land Rover. Rollins shouted to Tony just as he had slid into the Land Rover's back seat, "Grab the drone and follow us to the cabin."

Ivan had the gas pedal on the floor when, Mark yelled, "Take it easy as we approach the cabin, no need to announce we are coming." Ivan complied. Rollins continued, "Stop the car back from the place. If the agent's car still there, it means he is likely inside with Kole. Before we rush in, we need to have an idea of where he and Kole are located and what they are doing. Ivan, you take the front and be ready to break in if anything makes you think there is an immediate danger. I'll go left around to the back and Boris you go to the right—look, listen, and check windows. We will circle back to the front and decide our next moves."

The two seemed okay with Rollins taking the lead. Ivan replied. "Good plan—let's do it."

Ivan stopped the SUV short of the cabin and turned it sideways blocking the drive. They didn't want Jason's arrival in the Lexus to alert the agent. The three men took crouching positions and began moving towards the house executing their plan. Rollins pointed out the agent's car. Ivan and Boris nodded.

When the three reconvened at the front of the house, Boris reported seeing one window that was completely covered by foil. They agreed that was probably where Kole was being held. Otherwise, they heard nothing and saw no sign of the FBI guy. Nevertheless, because the car was there, they had to assume the agent was somewhere inside. They would go in with guns drawn. Rollins drew his small snub-nosed 38 Smith & Wesson revolver from his ankle holster. The Miami men had large automatics. They agreed that when they entered the cabin, Rollins would cover the left half of the front room and Boris would take the right side. That would leave Ivan free to go for Kole.

Ivan checked the front door. The lock was flimsy. On signal, he kicked the door open and the three rushed in. The large room was unoccupied, but there was a voice calling from the rear of the cabin.

"Help! Help! Somebody help!"

Ivan shouted, "Kole, where are you?"

"I'm in the back room!" After a second, Kole recognized the voice. Astonished, he yelled, "Ivan? Is that you?

Ivan didn't answer. He slammed his beefy shoulder against the door with Boris right behind him. It caved in crashing into the room as the two men clambered over it. Ivan scanned the room with his automatic in hand, asking under his breath, "Are you alone?"

"Yes. I'm okay. Just get me out of here!"

Seeing Kole chained like an animal, Ivan put his weapon away and dropped to his knees looking angrily at the restraint around Kole's ankle. "Who did this to you?"

"A guy who claimed to be an FBI Agent."

Boris returned to the land Rover and retrieved a rather serious looking tool bag that he sat down on the floor next to Kole. Ivan looked up at him and nodded toward the Kole's ankle. Boris selected one of his metal cutting tools and had the restraint off in less than a minute. Ivan stood, patted Boris on the back and said, "Is good!"

A little out of breath from their run up the drive, Tony arrived with Ella and Jason. Ella grabbed Kole and hugged him. "Thank God you are safe! We were going out of our minds—worried that you were injured or lying dead in some ditch."

Spotting an open package of baloney and a half eaten loaf of bread next to Kole's chair, Jason joked, "See Ella, I told you there was nothing to worry about. He has been eating high on the hog!"

Kole grinned. "I never want to see another baloney sandwich in my life. But I'm fine. Some dumb guy claiming to be an FBI agent drugged me. He stuck me with something as I was walking back to town. The next thing I knew, I was here chained to this place. He wanted me to give him the diary."

Kole noticed Rollins. Jason seeing the questioning expression on their friend's face explained, "This is Mark Rollins. Your mother called him, and he has been helping us look for you. If it hadn't been for him, your rescue would not be happening right now. And he is helping us with our search for the stolen Atlanta shipment. I'll tell you everything later."

Rollins added, "The man who has been holding you is Agent Walter M. Anderson. He is FBI, but we think he is not acting in an official capacity. His car is still parked out front. So, the important question is, where is he now?"

Kole said, "I don't know. I couldn't see anything from this room. I heard the door open and close, so I know he went out. Then I heard what sounded like a motorbike."

"A motorcycle! That's why we didn't know he had left Bat Cave, but why? Kole, did he say anything that might give us a clue?"

"The man was obsessed about the diary. That's why he kidnapped me. He wanted me to get it for him. And if I didn't, he threatened to take it from Jason and Ella. He's dangerous." Looking at his two friends, Kole continued, "I was afraid he might hurt the two of you."

Suddenly it hit Mark, and he shouted, "We need to return to the cottage, and I mean right now!"

Rollins, along with Tony and the students, began moving toward the cabin's door to leave, but Ivan stopped Kole, clutching his arm. "No, your uncle said to bring you to him—no stops! He wants to make sure you are not injured—have his doctor look you over."

Rollins turned around to face them. "What about the police? Kole must report his kidnapping."

"No good!" Ivan snapped forcefully. "No police, we do not do that. A Mrázek does not go to cops, ever!"

Tony countered, "You can't let that guy, Anderson, get away with this."

Boris smiled, looked at Tony and said, "Oh he won't!"

Kole resisted, "I can't go to Miami now. I need to be here with my friends."

Ivan didn't raise his voice, but you knew his orders were non-negotiable. "You got no choice. But I can have you back here tomorrow if your uncle okays it. Our plane is at the airport. I'll call the pilots so it will be ready to go as soon as we get there. So, let's get moving."

Rollins said, "Look, we can't wait any longer. We must get back to the cottage! Kole, just go with Ivan. We will get you back here tomorrow. I promise."

CHAPTER 39

The Heist

Shortly before Rollins' Lexus had arrived in Bat Cave to begin the search for the agent's car, Anderson, dressed in all black, wearing a typical biker's leather jacket and a balaclava, slipped on his helmet and adjusted the straps. He mounted the Royal Enfield INT650, pushed the starter button, and headed for the B&B and its adjacent cottage. The Enfield reminded him of the vintage motorcycles he rode when he was younger. He missed kicking off the motor to fire up the engine, the way bikers did before manufacturers added electric starters.

Once he hit the highway, the feeling of being on a bike, with the air rushing by, transported him back in time. He felt twenty years younger. Suddenly, he hit a pothole and that brought him back to the present. He decided to stop asking—it was time to just take the book.

He began taking stock of the current situation and planning his next steps. As an FBI agent, he had been taught the importance of visualization and mentally practicing plans of action. The success of a plan, even one's life, could depend on the 'what ifs' mentally dealt with in advance. He began to consider the boy in his cabin.

What the hell am I going to do with him— throw him off a cliff or push him into one of the thousands of waterfalls or deep lakes in these mountains? I've killed plenty of men and don't have a problem making it look like an accident. But then he is an illegal alien. The boy cannot do anything to me! When this is over, it is no sweat, I can just let the kid go.

Satisfied with his plan for dealing with Kole, his thoughts turned to the diary, the cottage, and its occupants.

Most likely, one or both students would be in the place. The thing to do is to do it fast. Bust in the door. Subdue the first student I come to. Slap the duct tape over number one's eyes and put restraints on hands and feet. Use the gun to control the second student if there. Put restraints on number two. Cover his or her eyes with more duct tape. Keep my mouth shut so they can't use the sound of my voice to identify me. Even with the balaclava covering my face, keep visual observation of me at a minimum. Find the book. Ransack the place taking every-thing of value that is easy to carry—make it look like just another opportunistic robbery.

He almost blew a curve. The winding mountain road would have been a fun ride, but he had to concentrate on business. Contingency. He needed a contingency plan. He ran different ideas through his mind, but they always came back to the same thing, kill them—a murder suicide. The more he thought about it, the more he liked the idea. It was simpler. It was a sure thing. No one knows about the book. It had been their secret. He got that much out of the Mrázek brat. As he thought about it, they probably do not lock the door. But even if they did, he knew how to unlock it without leaving a trace. First, shoot the girl. Then the boy, making it look like a murder-suicide. It was easy, and he knew how. He was only carrying a twenty-two automatic but that was perfect for a job like this. It did not make a lot of noise, yet one twenty-two caliber bullet in the right place kills a person dead—instantly.

He liked the plan.

CHAPTER 40

Missing Book

"Tony, make this a short trip."

"Sure thing, Mr. R."

Jason could feel Rollins' concern, but he didn't understand it. "Why the rush to get back to the cottage, Mr. Rollins?"

"My gut tells me we need to return. When I heard that the agent had changed his mode of transportation, especially to one we would never have expected—a motorcycle—my little gray cells started to tingle. Where did you leave the book?"

Jason answered, "I don't remember. Why?"

Rollins explained, "I think maybe he has gone after it."

"Oh no!" cried out Ella. "The table, I left the book on the table."

"Ella, don't worry," Jason assured her. "The diary is not important anymore. Not without that secret message we found."

Ella started crying. Stuttering, she managed to mutter, "I put it in the book!"

Rollins comforted her. "Ella, we don't know that he will break in and steal the book. We don't know for sure that he was even on his way to the cottage. My intuition is not always that good."

The rest of the drive to the cottage was a silent, anxious one. It felt like everyone was holding their breath.

∽

Agent Anderson could not believe his luck—no one was there. It took him only seconds to breach the door's lock. And there it was, across the room on a table in clear view. There was no mistaking the diary. It looked just as he had expected, and it matched the image he had seen on the video of Jason McConnell in the library. He looked around for something more to take. He wanted to make the book theft look like an ordinary robbery—some kid looking for drugs or something he could sell. Anderson was frustrated by the lack of anything of value other than a computer—actually two laptop computers. He grabbed both and left. "No reason to push my luck," he muttered to himself.

Later, as Tony drove the Lexus into the cottage parking space, there was an audible gasp from Ella. The door stood open. Jason was out of the car and in the cottage before the car had come to a complete stop. He was just standing in the middle of the room staring at the empty table when Rollins and Tony along with Ella had followed him in. He turned to face them and shouted, "He took it and the computers, too!"

Ella was holding back tears, and Jason slumped into a chair at the table.

Rollins stood still, thinking.

Jason straightened up. "Can't we go after him?"

Mark Rollins shook his head. "No. Look guys, this is not the end of the world. And it definitely is not the time to run off half-cocked chasing Anderson. He has the book and the message we found in its spine. But we don't need the book anymore, and we know what the secret message said. So, all we need to do now is develop a plan of action. My suggestion is that we get away from the crime scene's influence and map out the steps we are going to take next. Let's go to across to the main house and see what the Applewood Manor's kitchen can put together for us. It's almost eight and no one has eaten since our picnic lunch in the car. While we have dinner, we can finalize our plan."

No one felt hungry until the Manor's staff brought out a large charcuterie board of local meats and cheeses and a salad of fresh vegetables that Rollins swore someone must have just run up from the garden. There was also fruit and freshly baked rolls. They did a lot more eating than thinking. When the staff started clearing the table, Rollins rose and suggested, "Let's move to the parlor and get serious about deciding what we are going to do next."`

As they walked, Jason stopped abruptly, staring at a framed object on the wall. The Manor's walls are a gallery of paintings. But this was not your typical art piece. It was the reproduction of an old hand drawn map that Rollins had seen on his earlier visit to the parlor. The date was 1865. There on the map was Academy Street. And someone had added a handwritten note near the bottom of the map. It read: *Academy is now Montford Avenue.* Jason shouted. "This is the Academy Street Corporal Walker was writing about—the name was changed to Montford Avenue!"

Ella said, "What—I don't understand."

Rollins was surprised that he hadn't noticed earlier. Jason was right. In 1865, the road now called Montford Avenue went by the name Academy Street. Sometime, probably around the turn of the century when the Montford area was being developed for residential use, the name was changed to Montford Avenue.

Ella asked, "What about the road we've been looking at. The Academy Street we were all ready to dig up?"

Rollins explained, "As Jason suggested, the city planners simply reused the name. The road they now call Academy Street has nothing to do with the buried gold."

Jason added gleefully with a raised eyebrow and a smile, "We've won. But our FBI agent friend doesn't know that, does he?"

CHAPTER 41

The Big Dig

Rollins spent most of the night on the phone. Confirming, negotiating, coordinating, and arranging. One of the calls was one he would have preferred not to make. It was to Signore Roberto Greco. Mark had decided that Kole's uncle was unlikely to be persuaded to return Kole to Asheville by a call from Mark Rollins, someone he had never met. On the other hand, a call from one mafia boss to another would be very persuasive. That proved to be the case, when Greco's consigliere called back half an hour later to tell Rollins it had been taken care of. Kole would be there by the time the sun came up.

Rollins remembered the first time he and Greco crossed paths. It was at the Palm Restaurant in Nashville:

> *Signore Greco was a quintessential caricature of a New York Godfather. He wore a cashmere coat over his shoulders like a cape. His hat was a fedora. He carried a silver tipped cane. His features were Italian, and he was ac-*

companied by two rather big men. His son, like Kole, had been missing. In this case, father and son were estranged and the son was a murder suspect. Greco didn't know me from Adam, but he knew I was somehow involved with his son's disappearance. I found his son, helped clear him, and patched up the father and son relationship. For that, I became a friend of his, and as far as the Don was concerned, my wish was his command. He owed me and whatever I wanted he or his people would provide. Or as one of his men told me—'Whatever yous want you get—know what I mean.' It was a friend-ship that I found very uncomfortable, but one, I must admit was useful at times.

Everything was arranged. And scheduled to take place tomorrow at 10:00 a.m. Eastern Time.

At 9:30 in the morning, they were all in the car. Mark Rollins sat in the front passenger seat. The three treasure hunters squeezed into the back seat although the roomy LS 460 Lexus did not require a lot of squeezing.

Montford Avenue was just around the block from the Applewood Manor. Tony drove past the corner grocery store and turned right heading northwest. This section of Montford ended at a wooded strip of land less than a mile ahead. On the other side of that tree-laden area was Klondyke Avenue. They could see the excavator ahead. As they got closer, the barriers came into view and then the yellow tape that read: *KEEP OUT—UNITED STATES DEPARTMENT OF THE*

TREASURY. The dig site had been closed off to the public and heavily armed guards were stationed around the perimeter. Tony parked as close to the excavation area as possible.

As they got out of the car, Treasury Officers, Elizabeth Rodríguez and Chris Lee, met them. The officers introduced themselves, shaking hands all-around, but also verifying identities. The three would be treasure hunters also saw the armored truck parked not far away. All three seemed awestruck. Each thinking the same thought, "It is really happening!" Rodriguez seemed to be in charge. Speaking to the three she said, "We are ready to dig, but we had clear instructions that we were not to so much as put a spade in the dirt before you were here." The three friends, partners, didn't speak but all of them were smiling—big smiles. Ella finally managed to say, "If I faint, somebody catch me." At that, Jason and Kole laughed.

The 304E2 CAT Excavator's shovel was poised over a spot where the ground was sunken. It was what was left of the old Confederate battlement where CSA soldiers hunkered down ready to face the enemy, Union solders expected to advance from Genny's Creek. It was an advance that never came. And the abandoned battlement served as a ready hole in which General Welch's men would bury the Atlanta gold shipment. Now one hundred and fifty years later, Treasury Officer Chris Lee, holding a deep-reach detector, said to the group, "This is where we are going to dig. There is something here and this detector returned an atomic weight of 196.96657. I guess you three know what that is."

Kole answered. It came out first as a whisper, "Gold." And then as a shout, "GOLD!" Despite the instrument's validation the three were unbelievably tense. They would believe it when they saw it.

Officer Lee was positioned at the edge of the deepening hole watching as the excavator pulled out more dirt. Suddenly, he straightened and yelled, "We have hit pay dirt! He did a little jig—a weak imitation from the *Sierra Madre* movie. Of course, they all ran to the pit to look down. The excavator operator removed the bucket from the hole. They could see several wooden crates at the bottom. One was broken and spilling out of its side, they saw what looked like bars of solid gold. "Eureka!" shouted Jason. Then his two beaming teammates joined him in a group hug.

As a newbie at the Treasury, Chris Lee had been assigned to the Philadelphia Mint and his duties included the handling of gold bullion. He explained, "We are sending down a couple of men and they will start bringing the gold up." Looking at the bars at the bottom of the pit, he continued, "I would say the bars are bigger than today's standard twelve and half pound size. We call those 'Good Delivery Bars' in the international market. What's down there looks like more like the twenty-five pounders common in the eighteen hundreds. They are heavy for their size so we will bring them out one bar at a time and move each directly to the armored truck. "

Kole pleaded, "Can we help?" Lee looked to Officer Rodríguez for an answer.

After a pause, she said, "I don't see why not! Sure, you can. You three form a bucket brigade to pass the bars to the armored vehicle. Jason, I understand you found the diary that led us to this treasure. So, you will be first. As the bar is passed up, you take it and then hand it off to Ella. Ella, you pass it to Kole. And Kole, you give it to the armored truck officer. Chris, you are the chain of command witness and responsible for the count on our end."

Mark Rollins and Tony had moved to the Lexus. They were leaning against the side of the car, watching. Tony remarked, "I guess we don't each get one of those bars for services rendered."

Mark replied, "Nope! This one is strictly pro bono."

"You know Mr. R, that gold does not really bother me one bit. Watching all this just makes me feel good."

"You will feel even better when I tell you what Mycroft negotiated for those three kids. They don't know it yet, but each one has just become a multi-millionaire. I had asked Mycroft to get a ten percent tax free finder's fee for each of them. He went in asking for fifteen. The government negotiated it down to twelve and a half percent. That means that each of those three young people will be getting four million five hundred thousand dollars from the United States Treasury. And that's not all. Kole Mrázek gets a green card, officially known as a Permanent Resident Card, allowing him to live and work permanently in this country."

Meanwhile, across town, Agent Anderson, was overseeing his own excavation. This one was on a vacant lot at the west end of Academy Street. He, too, like Rollins, had been busy last night. After returning to the cabin and finding his prisoner gone, he decided it was time to move fast.

Although the more he thought about it, he really was in the clear up until now. No one could prove he took the diary, and Kole was still an illegal alien. Nevertheless, it was time to get the job done—dig up the gold and get out of Asheville. Actually, his plan was to get out of the States all together and he had already made the arrangements. He had a plane at the airport ready to take on the cargo and make the flight out of the country. The pilot, Josh Kane, was ex-military. He had flown many clandestine flights for the FBI and CIA. But when business was slow, the pilot took jobs from some of the very people who could be targets of either agency. Anderson trusted him and Josh was a man who knew how to avoid customs and keep his mouth shut—for a price.

Anderson had managed to track down the rental equipment manager of Mountain High Cat in Asheville. FBI credentials carry a lot of weight. That, plus an agreement to pay a five thousand dollar premium, was all it took to get the manager to agree to have a mini-excavator on the dig site by ten-thirty in the morning. Anderson also hired for an operator and a couple of strong but low level construction workers by agreeing to pay double their standard hourly rate. Academy Street was a dead end just as the narrow slip of paper the student had found had described. And there appeared to be a low spot, the Civil War battlement Anderson had concluded. He had not been able to determine who owned the vacant lot. But he wasn't worried. He didn't really expect anyone to question what was going on at the dig site—at least for a couple of hours. If they did, he would whip out his FBI badge and explain that the excavation was part of on an ongoing investigation.

The two construction workers had shown up, so Anderson had manpower to load the found gold into his rental truck. Now the mini-excavator and operator were ready to dig. The machine could dig as deep as sixteen feet. But excavators were not around in 1865. So, Anderson thought the gold would be down about four feet or six at the most.

He gave the signal and the excavator bit into the soil. Anderson watched intently. There was a metallic taste in his mouth. For just a second, he almost believed he could taste the gold that he was sure was only a few feet away. As the machine lifted more dirt and set it aside, the agent realized the dig had gone past four feet. He looked at the dirt pile, to make sure the gold was not in it. After an hour they were at six feet and had found nothing. Anderson was agitated. "It has to be there!" He was risking everything. It just had to be there! Maybe topsoil had been added since 1865. He signaled to keep digging. At eight feet, the mechanical shovel scraped on something. Anderson didn't wait. Mad with anticipation, he signaled to pull the shovel out. He grabbed a spade from a worker standing close by, jumped in and started digging at the bottom of the pit. Blinding anger erupted in him when his spade struck only rock—solid rock. The shovel had scraped against the face of a rock! He was muttering, slashing out with the spade—delivering pounding and stabbing blows to the wall of the dig—loose packed landfill laid down when the area was developed in the sixties. Then suddenly and without any warning, the walls caved in, burying FBI Agent Walter M. Anderson under tons of earth.

Anderson's hired men tried to save him but shovel for shovel the caving soil matched their desperate efforts. It was as though Heaven and Earth had considered the evidence and rendered their decision. For Agent Anderson, it was— *Forever Over.*

Karma:
The belief that one's fate is determined
by the sum of their prior actions.

THE END

ABOUT APPLEWOOD MANOR

Applewood Manor
Circa 1912
62 Cumberland Circle
Asheville, North Carolina

A pplewood Manor is located in the Montford Area Historic District of Asheville just a short walk to the heart of downtown Asheville. The Manor sits on a knoll surrounded by just over an acre of giant wild cherries, apple trees, oaks, pines, maples, and a variety of flora. It is just 3 miles from the breathtaking Biltmore Estate, a short 10-minute drive to the Blue Ridge Parkway and an ideal gateway to all the area's best routes for cycling and other outdoor adventures. Applewood Manor is modeled after properties like the Soho House with a blend of classic and contemporary décor delivering a more boutique hotel-like guest experience. The owners describe their mission for the historic inn this way:

> Our goal is to deliver the most differentiated and overall best bed & breakfast ("B&B") experience available in Asheville. But we aren't stopping there. Our long-term aspiration is to elevate our guest experience to be regarded as one of the top B&B properties anywhere in the world. While we are indeed a true bed & breakfast and not a hotel, our guests will find many aspects of their stay will compare favorably or exceed that of fine hotels. In many ways, we are endeavoring to create a new type of lodging experience to address rapidly changing guest preferences for more intimate and authentic environments without asking guests to forgo high-end amenities and thoughtfully curated luxurious spaces. Perhaps we are on the vanguard of creating a new sort of lodging category that we are calling "the bed and breakfast style boutique hotel." We invite you to be a part of our journey and share part of your story with us

While Applewood Manor is one of the longest continuously operating bed and breakfast style hotels in Asheville, more than a hundred years ago it started out as a personal residence. The original owner of this perfect specimen of a New England Colonial Revival home was Captain John Adams Perry.

Captain Perry was the classic army brat. He was born in Leavenworth, Kansas during his father's deployment to the base. He came from a long line of military men and heroes. His father, Alexander James Perry, went on to become a Brigadier General. Perhaps the most famous of the Perry men was Commodore Oliver Hazard Perry, the Naval hero who defeated the British Navy on Lake Erie in the War of 1812. While the Perry men served throughout the nation and abroad, their family roots were in Rhode Island, Connecticut, and New York. They were New Englanders.

When 44-year-old Captain Perry was disabled in 1903 during his Army service in the Philippines, he retired to Asheville for his health with his wife, Charlotte, and daughter, Anne. While his exact medical condition is not known, he probably suffered some type of lung damage, possibly tuberculosis. He purchased the site for his home on Cumberland Circle in 1908. The site is on the northern edge of what is now the Montford Area Historic District adjacent to downtown Asheville.

Perry hired the Asheville architect, William Henry Lord, to design the residence. The original architectural house plans with changes and notations in pencil are over 100 years old and remain with the home today. The house was completed in 1912. Perry's strong family history and ties to New England are evident in his architectural choice. The Early New England Style Colonial Revival is a two story structure of frame construction with a stone masonry foundation, cedar shake siding featuring a pediment entrance supported on Doric columns and flanking porches. The foundation was laid by the same stonemasons who worked on the Biltmore Estate. The floors are pine throughout.

Captain Perry has been characterized as a charming man who was amused by the children in the Montford neighborhood. He was to have delighted them by making kites and whittling windmills out of red cedar. He added a captain's walk to the west roof ridge reached through a skylight so he could watch the weather and survey Montford from high atop the knoll on which the house sits. When Captain John Adams Perry died in 1939, his daughter, Anne, and her husband, Dr. Eugene M. Carr, continued to live in the house until 1950. In 1987, the fourth owners converted the property to a bed and breakfast inn and christened it Applewood Manor. In 2020, Stephen and Robin Collins purchased the property and began a major remodeling and redecorating project to elevate the property to an elite class. They repositioned the Manor as an event B&B site with emphasis on Cycling, Culinary Experiences and Business Leadership and Management training.

Stephen Collins is a long-time software technology entrepreneur and leader with over three decades of global business experience. A former elite amateur competitive cyclist, Stephen remains an active member of the cycling community through his global cycling organization, Velo Roussillon, long term support of the USA Cycling Development Foundation and other related endeavors. Stephen is also an owner of AS IS NYC, a craft beer bar and restaurant in New York City. Robin began her career as a commercial interior designer in New York *City*. She is responsible for breakfast service as well as the yummy fresh-baked homemade cookies placed in every guest room. Over the last 25 years, Robin has become an outstanding bread baker whose efforts guests will surely enjoy during their stay. In addition to hundreds of hours practicing in her in-home bakery, she has taken baking courses at The French Culinary Institute in New York City along with many other classes and workshops in the USA and Europe.

Under Stephen's and Robin's stewardship, the Applewood Manor has been accepted as a member of the Select Registry. For fifty years the Select Registry has served as a seal of approval travelers can trust. The stamp of approval tells travelers that Applewood Manor is exceptional and unique, with one-of-a-kind setting, authentic experiences, local connections and flavors—with people who are genuinely honored to take great care of their guests.

ABOUT THE AUTHOR

 M. Thomas (Tom) Collins writes from his home in Franklin, Tennessee, where his characters come to life and frequent familiar places in the bucolic middle Tennessee landscape and the majestic mountains of Western North Carolina.

His book *Exploring Asheville—Its History Attractions, Mysteries, Ghosts, and Tall Tales* earned the top spot as the 2022 winner in the regional literature category at both the Independent Press Awards and the NYC Big Books Awards. Also winning in the Big Book Awards was his novel, *Beyond Visual Range*, as a 2022 Distinguished Favorite in Military Fiction.

A pioneer entrepreneur of the information technology industry, Tom is now retired from the commercial world and devotes his time to creating his mystery series, Mark Rollins Adventures and authoring his short stories about Asheville and Western North Carolina. You will find his books in your favorite neighborhood bookstore or online source. His books are available in print, digital and audio formats.

Tom Collins is available for selected readings and lectures.
To inquire about a possible appearance, contact the author at
www.authortomcollins.com

A BONUS SELECTION FROM THE
AWARD WINNING NOVEL,
BEYOND VISUAL RANGE,
A MARK ROLLINS ADVENTURE.

CHAPTER 1

Reaper Squadron

The 65th Special Operations Squadron is an air force unit based at Hurlburt Field, Florida. The squadron is composed of combatant commanders with intelligence, surveillance, reconnaissance (ISR), and precision strike capabilities. What makes these air force warriors different is that they do not climb into the aircraft they fly. Those aircrafts are often thousands of miles away, stationed around the globe. These are the men and women who fly the air force's fleet of Reaper drones—Remotely Piloted Aircraft or RPAs. The Reaper is the air force's newest iteration of the Predator drone. It is not, however, just a Predator by another name. It is bigger, flies higher and faster. It can stay in the theater longer and carry more armaments than its earlier cousins. It is a killing machine but spends most of its time searching, listening, and watching the enemy—harvesting intelligence across four combatant commands: Africa, Europe, the Middle East, and those units or agencies controlling Special Operations (SO). The term "special operations" is a euphemism. They are military, law enforcement, or intelligence units that are unconventional and carry out covert missions using nontraditional methods and resources. In the squad room, the airmen call them "our spooks."

The Reaper is flown by a two-person crew, a pilot and a sensor operator. The crew's cockpit never leaves the ground but functions every bit the same as a dual-piloted, wartime fixed wing fighter such as the F-14 Tomcat or the F-18 Hornet. The information flowing to the crew through the instruments, monitors, sensors, cameras, and satellites is too much for one person to manage. To avoid information overload, the pilot flies while the sensor operator mans the cameras and monitors the aircraft's telemetry and feedback systems. The crew multitasks to maintain situational awareness and accomplish their mission. Attack or destroy missions always involve a third person in addition to the crew. The clearance to engage the target is given or withheld by secret message or code from an out-of-cockpit mission commander up the chain of command, be it a first lieutenant right up through the president of the United States.

The MQ-9 Reaper cockpit is a windowless and soundproof air-conditioned flight deck built inside a battle-ready mobile metal container designed to be quickly deployed where needed. Inside, there is no sense of being in sunny, warm Florida.

⁂

Today, before dawn, over their Florida base, things were proceeding routinely. The mission was not routine, however. Not that any mission that involved flying over hostile territory was ever routine. The closest thing to it would have been intelligence gathering. This was a search and destroy mission. The pilot and sensor operator sitting side by side, both women were in uniform, and, because of the chill of the air conditioner, they were wearing standard issue jackets with the squadron insignia—six-sided rolling dice accompanied by its motto, *Scientia Fortuna Iuvat* (Fortune Favors the Bold). They were waiting. Waiting for a legal document, the tasking order, that would authorize the day's mission and provide critical information and instructions.

The tasking order came over the pilot's main computer screen. The pilot was Major Samantha Miller (aka Sam or "Sparks"). Major Miller earned the nickname Sparks as an F-35 fighter pilot before a terrible crash put her in a wheelchair, forcing her to leave airborne work to become a drone pilot. On her left was Senior Airman Rebecca Armistead. The mission, code name Splash-3, was to search and destroy three Iranian fast boats harbored together in the port of Latakia, Syria. The boats were part of a swarm that had harassed a US Navy vessel in the Mediterranean two days before. While not strategic in nature, the mission was to deliver a reminder that harassment of navy vessels would come with a price. The tasking order outlined threats to the mission, including hostile aircraft and vessels at sea that might be in or near the flight path. The order authorized an armament load of four Hellfire missiles and two GBU-16 Paveway laser-guided bombs. The Paveway bombs were listed as the primary ordnance for the mission. The Hellfire missiles were for defensive and contingent use.

The RPA, a Reaper MQ-9, assigned to the mission was stationed at Incirlik Air Base in Adana, Turkey. The Incirlik Aircraft Maintenance Squadron crew had prepared the Reaper, number 27 in the inventory, for launch and had loaded armaments according to tasking instructions sent directly to the airbase from the mission commander in charge of the engagement. In this case, mission command was one of the Special Operations Units.

The crew completed the standard preflight checklist. Satisfied, Major Miller took the controls of the MQ-9 and said, "Flight on." Within seconds the big Reaper drone, the ninth generation of the military's Predator drone family, was rolling and took much of the runway before going airborne. The sensor operator, ready to alert for any danger en route, had turned on the aircraft's cameras. Her monitor displayed a satellite view of the targets still docked hundreds of miles away.

Following protocol for an airstrike mission, the crew intended to maintain near radio silence. But, as the bird climbed, Pilot Miller, concern in her voice, remarked, "She seems to be flying heavy. What's the fuel load?"

Armistead responded, "Originally four thousand pounds, used two hundred, all normal."

"And the armaments?" questioned Miller.

"Showing normal full load weight, thirty-eight hundred pounds."

Puzzled, the pilot was silent for a minute, then said, "Seems a bit strange. We took a lot of runway for a normal load."

Referring to her sensors, the airman replied, "Nothing unusual indicated over here."

Miller's questions answered, conversation between the pilot and sensor operator ceased. There were ears everywhere and their safety and the mission's success were enhanced by stealth practices.

Thirty-seven minutes into the flight, speaking into her headphone, Armistead said, "Our flight time to the 'Go–No Go' location is seventeen minutes. All conditions normal."

One minute after the rendezvous with the designated location, twenty miles out and forty-five thousand feet over the Mediterranean Sea, the Go Code flashed on the sensor operator's main display. "We have clearance to engage Splash-3."

Major Miller responded, "Positioning."

Thirty miles away, ten miles inland from the crew's target, a CNN reporter, Jimmy Howell, and his producer, Liz Rosenberg, were having coffee on the balcony of the Al-Samman Hotel, a mile and a half from Tishreen University. Liz, the producer, stopped in midsentence and asked, "What was that?"

"What?" asked Jimmy.

"That bright flash! In the sky. Didn't you see it?"

Jimmy looked up.

"There it is again!" yelled Liz. The image faded.

She said, "Jimmy, people all over the place have been reporting seeing those lights and flashes. There is a story here, I just know it. Something is going on up there in space!"

"What? Do you think it's us?" Jimmy asked. "A secret weapon maybe, a super laser or something?"

"If it's a weapon, I hope it *is* us!" replied Liz. "I tell you, Jimmy, I smell a story."

Airman Armistead said, "Splash-3 laser lock complete."

Miller, without hesitation, threw the switch and voiced the away command for a deployed laser bomb, "Paveway-one, away!" A sudden change in the artificially created horizon on their display as the big Reaper rocked right surprised the crew; the air speed ticked up.

"What the hell?" shouted the pilot. "What did we just drop? Whatever it was, I'm sure as hell it wasn't what it was supposed to be. That was no Paveway laser bomb!"

The ordnance dropped, falling behind the Reaper. It ignited and flashed ahead, outrunning its surrogate mother ship. The front nose camera of the Reaper whited out from the intense bright flame of a rocket engine as it surged ahead of the drone.

The airman yelled, "It's a damn missile—a big one! That's no Hellfire—too big."

Pilot Miller, keeping her composure, responded, "What about our target?"

"The missile is going to fly right over it. What do we do now?" shouted Armistead.

Anger rising, Miller realized that without any authorization, they had just deployed an unknown weapon headed for an unknown target. She knew they could be in serious trouble unless they stayed calm and made the right moves. Her fighter pilot training kicked in.

"We complete the mission. We drop our number two laser bomb, destroy Splash-3, and then decide what to do next. I just pray that this time we get what we expect—one thousand pounds of laser-guided ordnance."

The airman said, "But the missile?"

Miller's voice was at a shouting pitch. "It is not our damn missile. This bird is not configured for whatever that thing was. It could have come from anywhere or anything, other than us. You understand, Airman? We can't be credited for that. We dropped our thousand pounder, bomb one. It must have been a dud, fell away, or something. So, we dropped number two and completed our mission—Splash-3. There can't be any question about this! Got it?"

The sensor operator got it: *Keep our mouths shut. This never happened!*

"Okay Major, locked on target for number two bomb."

A prearranged laser from some on-land source was lighting their target, making it unnecessary for the drone to have a visual other than the satellite view of the target.

"Here goes nothing." The pilot threw the switch, "Paveway-two, away!"

Armistead tracked the ordnance as it glided down from forty-five thousand feet, miles out from its target—the center ship of the three fast boats docked side by side.

"Bull's-eye! We have bang. Splash-3 destroyed!"

"Okay," said Miller. "Now let's follow the trail of that missile."

"Roger," said Armistead.

The pilot maneuvered the Reaper for an inland course at an altitude of fifty thousand feet to maintain a stealth aspect.

"Can you ID what the missile hit?"

Only seconds passed before the nose camera picked up a raging fire. The sensor operator watched the satellite image of the growing smoke plume as it billowed skyward from the fire—the apparent point of the missile's impact. Studying the monitor, she said, "I can't see crap through our cameras. The smoke is too thick. But let me check the coordinates."

Her voice shook with the shocking realization, and she cried, "Oh, my god, it's a hospital!"

Miller began taking the Reaper down to a lower altitude, flying a winding circle around the site of the missile strike. "We need to put eyes on this. Take some pictures. I'm going down below the smoke cloud. There is no telling just how many people are dead or injured, but it has to be in the hundreds. The world is going to demand to know who did this!"

At three thousand feet, Armistead had the aircraft's cameras rolling, recording high definition details of the strike site when her console display indicated skin impacts—pings from ground fire.

"Too low, Major. We're taking small arms fire from the ground. There's something else. A bogey approaching. It's another drone. From the markings, it looks like an Iranian make."

Miller replied, "I've got the bogey on screen and avoiding intercept. Time to bug out."

Just as the Reaper began to climb, the bogey intercepted the drone and appeared to attempt to ram the Reaper. Unfortunately, the Iranian aircraft occupied the same space as the wash from the Reaper's turboprop engine at maxed RPMs as the big bird started to climb to its fifty-thousand-foot perch. The lift under the wings of the Iranian's airship was stripped away by the force. Before the remote operator of the attacking drone could recover, it stalled, crashing into a building near the hospital.

As she maneuvered the Reaper away from the missile strike, Miller said, "Rebecca, we've been had. The spooks are up to some dirty work. If we let them get away with it, we take the rap. That thing flew like a cruise missile. It was a programmed weapon. If it did come from under our wing, it was programmed to hit that hospital before we ever left the tarmac. Damned spooks at Incirlik must have jerry-rigged it, replacing our number one laser bomb. If we are tagged with this, the consequences could be catastrophic and you can kiss your career in the United States Air Force goodbye. We'll be damned lucky to stay out of jail. To save our butts, we need to find out what happened at Incirlik. Until we do, we need to stick to our story. As far as we are concerned, all we know right now is that we threw the switch to deploy the first Paveway laser bomb, which we assume fell away—a dud. So, we dropped the second one. We did our job—Splash-3! Then we investigated the missile strike. Agreed?"

"Agreed, Major. All the way!"

CPSIA information can be obtained
at www.ICGtesting.com
Printed in the USA
JSHW012108021222
34209JS00002B/2/J